Moby-Dick

HERMAN MELVILLE

Moby-Dick
or, The Whale

PRESENTED BY

Jan Needle

ILLUSTRATED BY

Patrick Benson

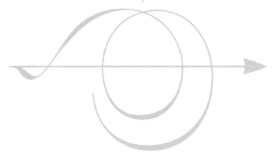

A Note by Jan Needle. . . . The story you are about to embark on is taken from the enormous novel published in 1851 by a former sailor named Herman Melville. For reasons of length, it has been edited — cut to the bone, one might even say — with passages of summary and commentary set in italics for the sake of clarity. Although Melville's novel is a work of fiction, he presented it as the true account of the extraordinary last voyage of the whaling ship *Pequod*, written by a sailor known only as Ishmael — the name of an outcast and wanderer in the Bible. Much of the original is long and rambling, even obscure, while other parts are wonderfully exciting. For Ishmael is not just a humble seaman but a survivor and a thinker who sees great significance in what happens to the ship.

There are echoes, in the manuscript, of other famous disasters in the whaling trade. In 1820, for instance, the Nantucket ship *Essex* was rammed and sunk by a furious sperm whale — an extremely rare occurrence. Her twenty officers and men set out in three small boats to try to reach the coast of South America, thousands of miles away; only eight survived. For Melville, who heard it from the son of the *Essex*'s first mate, the tragedy of a ship sent to destroy whales being destroyed by one itself was heavy with dark and secret meanings.

As Ishmael, Melville tells us about a whaling captain who is "a terrible old man," "mad" and "tragic." His name is Ahab—a wicked name, according to the text, and the name of a king who did great wrong in the sight of the Lord, according to the Bible. Ahab lost his leg fighting a whale that seems to him the embodiment of evil, despite the fact—or perhaps because of it—that unlike any other, this whale is white. What's more, Captain Ahab is certain that the attack was deliberate and is prepared to go to any lengths to get revenge.

Although the owners of the *Pequod*—and her crew—think their ship sets sail to hunt and slaughter many whales, for the captain, we realize at last, there is only one worth catching. He sets out, simply, to destroy it or die in the attempt. It is the thing that drives him onward.

Ishmael is on the voyage, and he alone survives. But over the years, his account has become a classic that reveals a myriad of meanings, not just for America, but wherever people read about and ponder the mysteries of humankind. Each reader will bring new ideas, which others might dispute with equal fervor, and the commentary in this version inevitably presents my own perspective as an Englishman who knows and loves the book—and the sea—with passion. But Melville's novel of the whale named Moby-Dick is beyond time and place. It is a story for the world.

all me Ishmael. Some years ago, having little or no money in my purse, and nothing particular to interest me on shore, I thought I would sail about a little and see the watery part of the world. Whenever I find myself growing grim about the mouth; whenever it is a damp, drizzly November in my soul; whenever I find myself pausing before coffin warehouses—then, I account it high time to get to sea as soon as I can. This is my substitute for pistol and ball. With a philosophical flourish Cato throws himself upon his sword; I quietly take to the ship. There is nothing surprising in this. If they but knew it, almost all men, some time or other, cherish very nearly the same feelings towards the ocean with me.

C H A P T E R
O N E

Loomings

Why is almost every robust healthy boy with a robust healthy soul in him, at some time or other crazy to go to sea? Why upon your first voyage as a passenger, did you yourself feel such a mystical vibration, when first told that you and your ship were now out of sight of land? And still deeper the meaning of that story of Narcissus, who because he could not grasp the tormenting image he saw in the fountain, plunged into it and was drowned. That same image, we ourselves see in all rivers and oceans. It is the image of the ungraspable phantom of life; and this is the key to it all.

Now, when I say that I am in the habit of going to sea whenever I begin to grow hazy about the eyes, and begin to be over conscious of my lungs, I do not mean to have it inferred that I ever go to sea as a passenger. Passengers get sea-sick—grow quarrelsome—don't sleep of nights—do not enjoy themselves, as a general thing. Nor, though I am something of a salt, do I ever go to sea as a Commodore, or a Captain, or a Cook. No, I go as a simple

sailor, right before the mast, plumb down into the forecastle, aloft there to the royal mast-head. True, they rather order me about some, and make me jump from spar to spar, like a grasshopper in a May meadow, and at first, this sort of thing is unpleasant enough. But this wears off in time. Do you think the archangel Gabriel thinks anything the less of me, because I obey? Who ain't a slave? Tell me that.

Again, I always go to sea as a sailor, because they make a point of paying me for my trouble, whereas they never pay passengers a single penny that I ever heard of. On the contrary, passengers themselves must pay. But wherefore it was that after having repeatedly smelt the sea as a merchant sailor, I should now take it into my head to go on a whaling voyage, why it was exactly that those stage managers, the Fates, put me down for this shabby part—I cannot tell; yet, now that I recall all the circumstances, I think I can see a little into the springs and motives.

Chief among these was the overwhelming idea of the great whale himself. Such a portentous and mysterious monster roused all my curiosity. Then the wild and distant seas where he rolled his island bulk; the undeliverable, nameless perils; I love to sail forbidden seas, and land on barbarous coasts. By reason of these things, then, the great flood-gates of the wonder-world swung open, and in the wild conceits that swayed me to my purpose, two and two there floated into my inmost soul, endless processions of the whale, and, midmost of them all, one grand hooded phantom, like a snow hill in the air.

⌐Ishmael, having come to his decision, stuffs a shirt or two into his carpetbag and starts for Cape Horn and the Pacific. He sails first from New York to New Bedford, which by the 1850s was the world's greatest whaling port, and from there to the island of Nantucket, which he tells us was "the place where the first dead American whale was stranded" and from where the Native Americans ("the Red-Men") began the industry that by the time of his voyage was one of the country's greatest and richest. It was not for food that whales were hunted, but for products that were far more valuable — a strong and flexible hornlike substance known as whalebone and the oil obtained by boiling down their fat, or "blubber." Before the discovery of oil that could be pumped out of the ground, whaling provided the bulk of the world's lighting oil, as well as lubrication for machines.

⌐Whatever his reasons for obscuring his real name, Ishmael is almost certainly being less than frank about why he chooses to go whaling. For most sailors it was a job of last resort, with voyages that could last three or four years and pay so low that a whaleman could easily end up with nothing after the owners had taken money for lost or damaged gear and other deductions. Some said whaleships smelled worse than slavers, and merchant sailors could spot a whaler by its slowness and filthy aspect from miles away. While some young men might have shipped for romantic reasons (much as Ishmael claims he does), these were not real seamen (as he claims he is), and their desertion rate was enormous. On the far-flung Pacific islands where the young sailors disappeared ashore, their replacements were usually what were then looked upon as cannibals and savages. In New Bedford, Ishmael notes, he saw "actual cannibals chatting at street corners; savages outright; many of whom yet carry on their bones unholy flesh." These "Feegeeans, Tongatabooans, Erromanggoans, Pannangians, and Brighggians" made strangers stare. America, at this time, was still afflicted by the shameful practice of slavery, but men who worked on ships — even "actual cannibals" — were almost always free. Whatever else he is, Ishmael is in no way what would be called a racist nowadays. In New Bedford, at the Spouter Inn, he shares his lodgings (and therefore his bed) with a South Sea islander named Queequeg, who turns up very late because he was out selling shrunken heads but who quickly becomes Ishmael's greatest friend. Queequeg, who worships a little wooden god called Yojo which he carries in his seabag, is a man of premonitions and, on the whaling voyage, has a coffin made for him by the ship's carpenter. This coffin, when every other soul is lost, saves Ishmael's life. When they reach Nantucket, Queequeg insists, at the bidding of his little god, that Ishmael go alone to choose their ship. Since he knows nothing of the whaling business, this prospect fills him with foreboding. And rightly so, it will turn out. . . .

Now, this plan of Queequeg's, or rather Yojo's, touching the selection of our craft; I did not like that plan at all. I had not a little relied upon Queequeg's sagacity to point out the whaler best fitted to carry us and our fortunes securely. But as all my remonstrances produced no effect, I was obliged to acquiesce. Next morning early, leaving Queequeg shut up with Yojo in our little bedroom, I sallied out among the shipping. After much prolonged sauntering and many random inquiries, I learnt that there were three ships up for three-years' voyages—The Devil-dam, the Tit-bit, and the Pequod. I peered and pryed about the Devil-dam; from her, hopped over to the Tit-bit; and, finally, going on board the Pequod, looked around her for a moment, and then decided that this was the very ship for us.

Strange way to make a choice indeed. Strange choice. They end up as sailors on a godless ship, with a godless captain, embarking on a voyage of the damned. Ishmael's description of the ship is enough to make one's blood run cold. . . .

You may have seen many a quaint craft in your day, for aught I know;—square-toed luggers; mountainous Japanese junks; butter-box galliots, and what not; but take my word for it, you never saw such a rare old craft as this same rare old Pequod. She was a ship of the old school, rather small if anything; with an old fashioned claw-footed look about her. Her ancient decks were worn and wrinkled, like the pilgrim-worshipped flag-stone in Canterbury Cathedral where Becket bled. She was apparelled like any barbaric Ethiopian emperor, his neck heavy with pendants of polished ivory. She was a thing of trophies. A cannibal of a craft, tricking herself forth in the chased bones of her enemies. All round, her unpanelled, open bulwarks were garnished like one continuous jaw, with the long sharp teeth of the sperm whale, inserted there for pins, to fasten her old hempen thews and tendons to. Scorning a turnstile wheel at her reverend helm, she sported there a tiller; and that tiller was in one mass, curiously carved from the long narrow lower jaw of her hereditary foe. A noble craft, but somehow a most melancholy! All noble things are touched with that.

CHAPTER
TWO

The Ship

A noble craft, but most melancholy. . . . This, in his brief description, is perhaps the least chilling thing that Ishmael can find to say about the Pequod. He mentions pilgrims, Canterbury Cathedral, and the blood of Thomas à Becket who was murdered there, but does not tell us that the Pequod, or Pequot, a tribe of Native Americans, were exterminated a hundred years before; the name Pequod commemorates mass death. The area where the steersman works is described as "reverend," but the tiller is a jawbone. The ship, indeed, is festooned with trophies of slaughtered whales. She is "barbaric" and a "cannibal." ⟋ Ishmael's forebodings grow when he meets the two strange old men who own the boat. Both ex-captains, both Quakers, they are named Peleg and Bildad, and they perform a sort of crazy double act to swindle him into accepting far less for signing on the *Pequod* than he expected (and deserves). ⟋ Ishmael knows already that the payment system on these ships was done by "lays," or shares of the profits (if any) of the voyage, and that the greater the experience and usefulness of each man, the greater his "lay."

As a seaman, if not a whaling hand, Ishmael expects a 275th lay, and hopes— "considering I was of broad-shouldered make" *— he would be offered a 200th. In fact he gets a 300th. Compare this with Queequeg's, when he signs on later. Captain Peleg, uninterested in giving a "savage" his correct name, is impressed by his looks, however, and demands a demonstration of his skill.*

Without saying a word, Queequeg, in his wild sort of way, jumped upon the bulwarks, and poising his harpoon, cried out in some such way as this:—

"Cap'ain, you see him small drop tar on water dere? You see him? well, spose him one whale eye, well, den!" and taking sharp aim at it, he darted the iron right over old Bildad's broad brim, clean across the ship's decks, and struck the glistening tar spot out of sight.

"Quick, Bildad," said Peleg, "and get the ship's papers. We must have Hedgehog there, I mean Quohog, in one of our boats. Look ye, Quohog, we'll give ye the ninetieth lay, and that's more than ever was given a harpooneer yet out of Nantucket."

Ishmael is not the man to be jealous of his friend's triumph, though: he rejoices. His trusting nature has already led him to sign ship's articles, before Queequeg has even seen the Pequod — and without meeting his new captain. He has asked — but Peleg offers him no hope at all.

"Young man, he won't always see me, so I don't suppose he will thee. He's a grand, ungodly, god-like man, Captain Ahab; doesn't speak much; but, when he does speak, then you may well listen.

Mark ye, be forewarned; Ahab's above the common; Ahab's been in colleges, as well as 'mong the cannibals; been used to deeper wonders than the waves; fixed his fiery lance in mightier, stranger foes than whales. His lance! aye, the keenest and the surest out of all our isle! Oh! he ain't Captain Bildad; no, and he ain't Captain Peleg; *he's Ahab,* boy; and Ahab of old, thou knowest, was a crowned king!"

"And a very vile one. When that wicked king was slain, the dogs, did they not lick his blood?"

"Come hither to me—hither, hither," said Peleg, with a significance in his eye that almost startled me. "Look ye, lad; never say that on board the Pequod. Never say it anywhere. Captain Ahab did not name himself. 'Twas a foolish, ignorant whim of his crazy, widowed mother, who died when he was only a twelvemonth old. I know Captain Ahab well; I've sailed with him as mate years ago; I know what he is—a good man—not a pious, good man, like Bildad, but a swearing good man—something like me—only there's a good deal more of him. Aye, aye, I know that he was never very jolly; and I know that on the passage home, he was a little out of his mind for a spell; but it was the sharp shooting pains in his bleeding stump that brought that about, as any one might see. I know, too, that ever since he lost his leg last voyage by that accursed whale, he's been a kind of moody—desperate moody, and savage sometimes; but that will all pass off. And once for all, let me tell thee and assure thee, young man, it's better to sail with a moody good captain than a laughing bad one. So good-bye to thee—and wrong not Captain Ahab, because he happens to have a wicked name. Besides, my boy, he has a wife—not three voyages wedded—a sweet, resigned girl. Think of that; by that sweet girl that old man has a child: hold ye then there can be any utter, hopeless harm in Ahab? No, no, my lad; stricken, blasted, if he be, Ahab has his humanities!"

All things considered, then, Ishmael leaves the *Pequod* thoughtful, especially about the nature of the invisible and most mysterious Captain Ahab. Before the *Pequod* leaves Nantucket, there are several more disturbing omens, starting with a dockside meeting with a "ragged old sailor" who claims his name is Elijah (in the Old Testament, Elijah prophesies that Ahab will be destroyed) and who hints at many more dark secrets hidden in the captain's past.

And when, on the day of sailing, Ishmael thinks he sees some sailors running along the wharf ahead of him and Queequeg toward the ship, who should appear again, from out of the misty dawn, but Elijah. He comes up close behind them, claps his hand on Ishmael's shoulder, and speaks:

"Did ye see anything looking like men going towards that ship a while ago?"

Struck by this plain matter-of-fact question, I answered, saying, "Yes, I thought I did see four or five men; but it was too dim to be sure."

"Very dim, very dim," said Elijah. "Morning to ye."

Once more we quitted him; but once more he came softly after us; and touching my shoulder again, said, "See if you can find 'em now, will ye?"

"Find who?"

"Morning to ye!" he rejoined. "Oh, I was going to warn ye against— but never mind, never mind—it's all one; all in the family too;— sharp frost this morning, ain't it? Good bye to ye. Shan't see ye again very soon, I guess; unless it's before the Grand Jury." And with these cracked words he finally departed, leaving me, for the moment, in no small wonderment at his frantic impudence.

When they get onboard, Ishmael mentions the shadowy sailors, but Queequeg, it seems, did not even notice them. They exist, though, and later in the voyage, they are — very strangely — to reappear.

That very afternoon, the Pequod sets sail. Christmas is upon them, when pious Nantucket Islanders thank heaven for the birth of Christ, their Savior. Christmas or not, however, it is the day ordained for the Pequod to go earning, and earn she will. Peleg and Bildad were to stay onboard to steer her to the safety of the open sea (which will save them extra cash as well, in pilot fees), so Ahab lurks below — still a mystery, still unseen. Ishmael comforts himself that many merchant captains keep to their cabins at the start of voyages, drinking with their friends — but friendless Ahab is alone, of course, and certainly not drinking. Ishmael puts his bravest face on it but describes the farewell in terms of great foreboding. It is to be many, many days, in fact, and many, many miles, before he and his fellow whalemen have a sight of Ahab on the deck.

CHAPTER
THREE

Merry Christmas

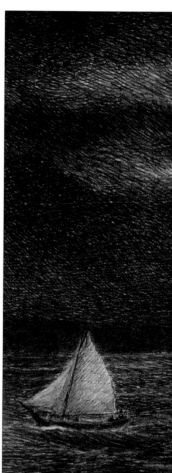

At last the anchor was up, the sails were set, and off we glided. It was a short, cold Christmas; and as the short, northern day merged into night, we found ourselves almost broad upon the wintry ocean, whose freezing spray cased us in ice, as in polished armor. The long rows of teeth on the bulwarks glistened in the moonlight; and like the white ivory tusks of some huge elephant, vast curving icicles depended from the bows.

Lank Bildad, as pilot, headed the first watch, and ever and anon, as the old craft deep dived into the green seas, and sent the shivering frost all over her, and the winds howled, and the cordage rang, his steady notes were heard,

"Sweet fields beyond the swelling flood,
Stand dressed in living green.
So to the Jews old Canaan stood,
While Jordan rolled between."

Never did those sweet words sound more sweetly to me than then. They were full of hope and fruition. Spite of this frigid winter night in the boisterous Atlantic, spite of my wet feet and wetter jacket, there was yet, it then seemed to me, many a pleasant haven in store; and meads and glades so eternally vernal, that the grass shot up by the spring, untrodden, unwilted, remains at midsummer.

At last we gained such an offing, that the two pilots were needed no longer. The stout sail-boat that had accompanied us began ranging alongside.

"God bless ye, and have ye in His holy keeping, men," murmured old Bildad, almost incoherently. "I hope ye'll have fine weather now, so that Captain Ahab may soon be moving among ye—a pleasant sun is all he needs, and ye'll have plenty of them in the tropic voyage ye go."

"Come, come, Captain Bildad; stop palavering,—away!" and with that, Peleg hurried him over the side, and both dropt into the boat.

Ship and boat diverged; the cold, damp night breeze blew between; a screaming gull flew overhead; the two hulls wildly rolled; we gave three heavy-hearted cheers, and blindly plunged like fate into the lone Atlantic.

Unlike many sailors who made their living in the hard and terrifying world of deep-sea whaling, Ishmael sees himself as a philosopher. He also knows that he and his fellows in the trade are outcasts of society in many ways, destined to marry "sweet, resigned girls" (like Ahab's poor young wife) and father children

CHAPTER FOUR

The Advocate

separated in age by three or four years (depending on the length of each voyage), who will grow up hardly seeing, or knowing, their absent fathers. This worries him, he says, as whaling has somehow "come to be regarded among landsmen as a rather unpoetical and disreputable pursuit," and he is "all anxiety to convince ye, ye landsmen, of the injustice hereby done to us hunters of whales." ‿ His attempt to set himself up as an "advocate" for whalemen, however, to present their case as a lawyer would have done, is somewhat spoiled by his inability to be completely serious. He admits that whaling was a "butchering sort of business," but excuses it by pointing out that famous military commanders are also butchers "of the bloodiest" — and are heaped with honors for it! ‿ As for the "alleged uncleanliness of our business," he claims that he could prove that whaleships rank among the "cleanest things of this untidy earth," then adds that the reeking, blood-drenched decks might in fact be filthy, but are incomparably better than a battlefield with its "unspeakable carrion." What's more, not only do soldiers return from their form of carnage to be feted and adored for their bravery while whalemen are shunned, but heroes who would march boldly up to a battery of guns would not be so brave when presented with a sperm whale's vast tail rising above their heads. Ishmael wants to have it both ways. . . . Taking the irony further, he also challenges "loyal Britons" to consider that when a king's head is solemnly anointed at his coronation (like a "head of salad"), the oil used is the product of the so-called vile, barbaric act of whaling. And to settle it beyond all doubt, he cites the "profoundest homage" paid to whale hunters by the whole world even while contumely is heaped upon them. "For almost all the tapers, lamps and candles that burn round the globe burn, as before so many shrines, to our glory!" Not so jokingly, Ishmael is well aware of the importance of whaling to the economy of America. Her fleet, he points out, is **upwards of seven hundred vessels; manned by eighteen thousand men; yearly consuming 4,000,000 of dollars; the ships worth, at the time of sailing, $20,000,000; and every year importing into our harbors a well reaped harvest of $7,000,000.** ⮑ What is more, he says, the whale ship is the pioneer of ferreting out the remotest and least known parts of the earth and has explored seas and archipelagos that have no charts, and where no Cook or Vancouver has ever sailed. He credits whalemen with freeing the west of South America from the "yoke of Old Spain" and with the establishment of democracy there. Australia, he asserts, was "given to the enlightened world" by the men who hunted whales, while "the uncounted isles of all Polynesia" were opened up to missionaries and merchants in the same way. ⮑ Even Japan, he points out — which in those days had a national policy of absolute secrecy and detachment from the wider world — was being slowly made "hospitable" because of enlightenment brought by whale ships. A very weird enlightenment, he might be hinting: the enlightenment of a massive exercise of bloody butchery. To drive home the point, perhaps — having built up a solid picture of a noble and important industry — Ishmael now decides it is time for his readership to face the agent of destruction who will bring the whole construction crashing down: his tragic captain. ⮑

*F*or several days after leaving Nantucket, nothing above hatches was seen of Captain Ahab. The mates regularly relieved each other at the watches, and for aught that could be seen to the contrary, they seemed to be the only commanders of the ship.

CHAPTER
FIVE

Ahab

Every time I ascended to the deck from my watches below, I instantly gazed aft to mark if any strange face were visible; for my first vague disquietude touching the unknown captain became almost a perturbation. This was strangely heightened at times by the ragged Elijah's diabolical incoherences recurring to me, with a subtle energy I could not have before conceived of. But whatever it was of apprehensiveness or uneasiness which I felt, yet whenever I came to look about me in the ship, it seemed against all warranty to cherish such emotions. For though the great body of the crew were a far more barbaric, heathenish, and motley set than any of the tame merchant-ship companies which my previous experiences had made me acquainted with, I ascribed this to the fierce uniqueness of that wild vocation in which I had embarked. It was especially the aspect of the three chief officers of the ship, the mates, which was calculated to allay misgivings, and induce confidence and cheerfulness in the voyage. Three better, more likely sea-officers and men, each in his own different way, could not readily be found, and they were every one of them Americans; a Nantucketer, a Vineyarder, a Cape man. Now, it being Christmas when the ship shot from out her harbor, for a space we had biting Polar weather, though all the time running away from it to the southward; and by every degree and minute of latitude which we sailed, gradually leaving that merciless winter, and all its intolerable weather behind us. It was one of those less lowering, but still grey and gloomy enough mornings of the transition, that as I mounted to the deck at the call of the forenoon watch, foreboding shivers ran over me. Reality outran apprehension; Captain Ahab stood upon his quarter-deck.

There seemed no sign of common bodily illness about him, nor of the recovery from any. He looked like a man cut away from the stake, when the fire has overrunningly wasted all the limbs without consuming them, or taking away one particle. His whole high, broad form, seemed made of solid bronze, and shaped in an unalterable mould, like Cellini's cast Perseus. Threading its way out from among his grey hairs, and continuing right down one side of his tawny scorched face and neck, till it disappeared in his clothing, you saw a slender rod-like mark, lividly whitish. It resembled that perpendicular seam sometimes made in the straight, lofty trunk of a great tree, when the upper lightning tearingly darts down it, and without wrenching a single twig, peels and grooves out the bark from top to bottom, ere running off into the soil, leaving the tree still greenly alive, but branded. Whether that mark was born with him, or whether it was the scar left by some desperate wound, no one could certainly say.

So powerfully did the whole grim aspect of Ahab affect me, and the livid brand which streaked it, that for the first few moments I hardly noted that not a little of this overbearing grimness was owing to the barbaric white leg upon which he partly stood. It had been fashioned from the polished bone of the sperm whale's jaw.

I was struck with the singular posture he maintained. Upon each side of the Pequod's quarter deck, there was an auger hole, bored about half an inch or so, into the plank. His bone leg steadied in that hole; one arm elevated,

and holding by a shroud; Captain Ahab stood erect,
looking straight out beyond the ship's ever-pitching
prow. Not a word he spoke; nor did his officers say
aught to him; but moody stricken Ahab stood
before them with a crucifixion in his face;
in all the nameless regal overbearing dignity
of some mighty woe.

Ahab's three mates, Ishmael recognizes, are "momentous men." They command the whaleboats — fast, double-ended twenty-five footers — and, armed with long, sharp whaling spears, appear to him like Gothic knights of old. All three boats — and another for the captain, on some whale ships — were constantly in readiness and would be swung overboard and dropped into the water the instant a whale was spotted from the mastheads. Each mate would steer his whaleboat, while his "squire," the harpooneer, would take the bow oar for the pursuit, often rowing madly many, many miles. When a whale was reached, the harpooneer had to drop his oar, jump around to face forward in the lightweight, unstable boat, pick up his harpoon, and throw it with every ounce of strength he could still summon up. If its barbs fixed in the whale's flesh, the creature was thereby attached, by an enormously long, strong rope, to the boat. If the whale raced off, the boat was towed at breakneck speed, sometimes well out of sight of watchers on the ship.

CHAPTER SIX

Knights and Squires

As if this was not dangerous enough, once the whale was attached to the harpoon line, the harpooneer and the mate had to change places — running from end to end of the crowded, pitching cockleshell — so that the mate could drive his spear into the whale when they could get close enough. It often took many thrusts before the lancer could find the heart, and the whales, although not generally aggressive even in this final struggle, destroyed many boats and many men in their wild thrashings. Another part of the harpooneer's job was to provide his knight with a fresh lance if the first one was lost or damaged. No surprise then that although of different classes and often of different races and religions, these men could form powerful bonds. Ishmael introduces them almost formally.

The chief mate was Starbuck, a native of Nantucket, and a Quaker by descent. He was a long, earnest man, and though born on an icy coast, seemed well adapted to endure hot latitudes, his flesh being hard as twice-baked biscuit. Starbuck had selected Queequeg for his squire.

Next was Tashtego, an unmixed Indian from Gay Head, the most westerly promontory of Martha's Vineyard, where there still exists the last remnant of a village of red men. To look at the tawny brawn of his lithe snaky limbs, you would almost have credited the superstitions of some of the earlier Puritans, and half believed this wild Indian to be a son of the Prince of the Powers of the Air. Tashtego was Stubb's squire.

Stubb was the second mate. Good-humored, easy, and careless, he presided over his whale-boat as if the most deadly encounter were but a dinner, and his crew all invited guests. When close to the whale, in the very death-lock of the fight, he handled his unpitying lance coolly and off-handedly, as a whistling tinker his hammer. Long usage had, for this Stubb, converted the jaws of death into an easy chair. What, perhaps with other things, made Stubb such an easy-going, unfearing man; what helped to bring about that almost impious good-humor of his; that thing must have been his pipe. For, like his nose, his short, black little pipe was one of the regular features of his face. When Stubb dressed, instead of first putting his legs into his trowsers, he put his pipe into his mouth.

The third mate was Flask, a short, stout, ruddy young fellow, very pugnacious concerning whales, who some- how seemed to think that the great Leviathans had personally and hereditarily affronted him; and therefore it was a sort of point of honor with him, to destroy them whenever encountered. They called him King-Post; because, in form, he could be well likened to the short, square timber known by that name in Arctic whalers.

Third among the harpooneers was Daggoo, a gigantic, coal-black negro-savage, with a lion-like tread. Suspended from his ears were two golden hoops, so large that the sailors called them ring-bolts, and would talk of securing the top-sail halyards to them. Daggoo retained all his barbaric virtues, and erect as a giraffe, moved about the decks in all the pomp of six feet five in his socks.

There was a corporeal humility in looking up at him; and a white man standing before him seemed a white flag come to beg truce of a fortress. Curious to tell, this imperial negro was the Squire of little Flask, who looked like a chess-man beside him. ⌒ The rest of the ship's company, Ishmael says, is also largely non-American — except for the officers — as was normal in the whaling fleet. The best whalemen were plucked off islands, and the very best were "Isolatoes," a word Ishmael coins for men who seem to have their own imagined continents inside their heads. These go with Ahab "to lay the world's grievances before that bar from which not very many of them ever come back." ⌒ And here he mentions "Black Little Pip," the Alabama slave boy who is desperate to come back to land again one day but most definitely will not. We will see him later, Ishmael tells us, on the grim *Pequod*'s forecastle, beating his tambourine as before long he will beat it in heaven with the angels. ⌒ We *do* see him playing for the *drunken* crew one *dreadful*, godless, merry night. Pip plays, then goes to hide and say a silent prayer. It is *not* answered. ⌒

By the time of Ishmael's voyage, the days of easy pickings for the whalers were long gone. Nantucket became supreme in the early decades of the eighteenth century, when they extended their offshore fishing much farther into the Atlantic Ocean. From the earliest days they had caught right whales, but now they equipped seagoing vessels to find and kill sperm whales, which were bigger and much richer in their yields. As the Nantucketers became more successful, the whales grew scarcer, and the length of voyage, and the distance sailed, extended rapidly. Around the turn of the nineteenth century, Nantucket ships pushed past Cape Horn into the Pacific Ocean. From then on, voyages of two, three, or even four years became commonplace. ⌐ So it is that one fine day — though still not many weeks at sea — Ishmael does his first turn at the mast-head, searching for the sperm whale's telltale spout. So it is that Captain Ahab, one fine afternoon, orders Starbuck to call all hands.

CHAPTER SEVEN

Moby Dick

"Sir!" said the mate, astonished at an order seldom or never given on ship-board except in some extraordinary case.

"Send everybody aft," repeated Ahab. "Mast-heads, there! come down!"

When the entire ship's company were assembled, and with curious and not wholly unapprehensive faces, were eyeing him, he cried:—

"What do ye do when ye see a whale, men?"

"Sing out for him!" was the impulsive rejoinder from a score of clubbed voices.

"Good!" cried Ahab, with a wild approval in his tones.

"And what do ye next, men?"

"Lower away, and after him!"

"And what tune is it ye pull to, men?"

"A dead whale or a stove boat!"

More and more strangely and fiercely glad and approving, grew the countenance of the old man. Ahab, now half-revolving in his pivot-hole, with one hand reaching high up a shroud, and tightly, almost convulsively grasping it, addressed them thus:—

"Look ye! d'ye see this Spanish ounce of gold?"—holding up a broad bright coin to the sun—"it is a sixteen dollar piece, men. D'ye see it? Mr. Starbuck, hand me yon top-maul."

Receiving the top-maul, he advanced towards the main-mast with the hammer uplifted in one hand, exhibiting the gold with the other, and with a high-raised voice exclaiming: "Whosoever of ye raises me a white-headed whale with a wrinkled brow and a crooked jaw; whosoever of ye raises me that white-headed whale, with three holes punctured in his starboard fluke—look ye, whosoever of ye raises me that same white whale, he shall have this gold ounce, my boys!"

"Huzza! huzza!" cried the seamen, as with swinging tarpaulins they hailed the act of nailing the gold to the mast.

"It's a white whale, I say," resumed Ahab, as he threw down the top-maul; "a white whale. Skin your eyes for him, men; look sharp for white water; if ye see but a bubble, sing out."

"Captain Ahab," said Tashtego, "that white whale must be the same that some call Moby Dick."

"Moby Dick?" shouted Ahab. "Do ye know the white whale then, Tash?"

"Does he fan-tail a little curious, sir, before he goes down?" said the Gay-Header deliberately.

"And has he a curious spout, too," said Daggoo, "very bushy, even for a parmacetty, and mighty quick, Captain Ahab?"

"And he have one, too, tree—oh! good many iron in him hide, too, Captain," cried Queequeg disjointedly, "all twiske-tee be-twisk, like him— him—" faltering hard for a word, and screwing his hand round and round as though uncorking a bottle—"like him—him—"

"Corkscrew!" cried Ahab, "aye, Queequeg, the harpoons lie all twisted and wrenched in him; aye, Daggoo, his spout is a big one, like a whole shock of wheat, and white as a pile of our Nantucket wool after the great annual sheep-shearing; aye, Tashtego, and he fan-tails like a split jib in a squall. Death and devils! men, it is Moby Dick ye have seen—Moby Dick— Moby Dick!"

"Captain Ahab," said Starbuck, who, with Stubb and Flask, had thus far been eyeing his superior with increasing surprise, "Captain Ahab, I have heard of Moby Dick—but it was not Moby Dick that took off thy leg?"

"Who told thee that?" cried Ahab; then pausing, "Aye, Starbuck; aye, my hearties all round; it was Moby Dick that dismasted me; Moby Dick that brought me to this dead stump I stand on now. Aye, aye," he shouted with a terrific, loud, animal sob, like that of a heart-stricken moose; "Aye, aye! it was that accursed white whale that razeed me; made a poor pegging lubber of me for ever and a day!" Then tossing both arms, with measureless imprecations he shouted out: "Aye, aye! and I'll chase him round Good Hope, and round the Horn, and round the Norway Maelstrom, and round perdition's flames before I give him up. And this is what ye have shipped for, men! to chase that white whale on both sides of land, and over all sides of earth, till he spouts black blood and rolls fin out. What say ye, men, will ye splice hands on it, now? I think ye do look brave."

"Aye, aye!" shouted the harpooneers and seamen, running closer to the excited old man: "A sharp eye for the White Whale; a sharp lance for Moby Dick!"

"God bless ye," he seemed to half sob and half shout. "God bless ye, men. Steward! go draw the great measure of grog. But what's this long face about, Mr. Starbuck; wilt thou not chase the white whale? art not game for Moby Dick?"

"I am game for his crooked jaw, and for the jaws of Death too, Captain Ahab, if it fairly comes in the way of the business we follow; but I came here to hunt whales, not my commander's vengeance. Vengeance on a dumb brute, that simply smote thee from blindest instinct! Madness! To be enraged with a dumb thing, Captain Ahab, seems blasphemous."

"Talk not to me of blasphemy, man; I'd strike the sun if it insulted me. But look ye, Starbuck, see yonder Pagan leopards—the crew, man, the crew! Are they not one and all with Ahab, in this matter of the whale? See Stubb! he laughs! See yonder Chilian! he snorts to think of it."

"God keep me!—keep us all!" murmured Starbuck, lowly.

But in his joy at the enchanted, tacit acquiescence of the mate, Ahab did not hear his foreboding invocation; nor yet the low laugh from the hold; nor yet the hollow flap of the sails against the masts, as for a moment their hearts sank in. For again Starbuck's downcast eyes lighted up with the stubbornness of life; the subterranean laugh died away; the winds blew on; the sails filled out; the ship heaved and rolled as before.

"The measure! the measure!" cried Ahab.

Receiving the brimming pewter, and turning to the harpooneers, he ordered them to produce their weapons. Then ranging them before him near the capstan, with their harpoons in their hands, while his three mates stood at his side with their lances, and the rest of the ship's company formed a circle round the group; he stood for an instant searchingly eyeing every man of his crew. Those wild eyes met his, as the bloodshot eyes of the prairie wolves meet the eye of their leader, ere he rushes on at their head.

"Drink and pass!" he cried, handing the heavy charged flagon to the nearest seaman. "The crew alone now drink. Round with it, round! Short draughts—long swallows, men; 'tis hot as Satan's hoof. Steward, refill!"

After this, Ahab makes his three mates cross their lances in front of him and seizes the sharp blades where they join. He twitches them suddenly, as if shocking them with "his own magnetic life." Then he orders the mates to become "cup-bearers" to their harpooneers, who detach the deadly blades from their harpoons and hold them point downward so that their sockets form drinking goblets. Then he tells the mates:

"So, so; now, ye cup-bearers, advance. The irons! take them; hold them while I fill!" Forthwith, slowly going from one officer to the other, he brimmed the harpoon sockets with the fiery waters from the pewter.

"Now, three to three, ye stand. Commend the murderous chalices! Bestow them, ye who are now made parties to this indissoluble league. Ha! Starbuck! but the deed is done! Drink, ye harpooneers! drink and swear, ye men that man the deathful whaleboat's bow—Death to Moby Dick! God hunt us all, if we do not hunt Moby Dick to his death!" The long, barbed steel goblets were lifted; and to cries and maledictions against the white whale, the spirits were simultaneously quaffed down with a hiss. Starbuck paled, and turned, and shivered. Once more, and finally, the replenished pewter went the rounds among the frantic crew; when, waving his free hand to them, they all dispersed; and Ahab retired within his cabin.

I, Ishmael, was one of that crew; my shouts had gone up with the rest; my oath had been welded with theirs; and stronger I shouted, and more did I hammer and clinch my oath, because of the dread in my soul.

Here, then, was this grey-headed, ungodly old man, chasing with curses a Job's whale round the world, at the head of a crew chiefly made up of mongrel renegades, and castaways, and cannibals—morally enfeebled also, by the incompetence of mere unaided virtue or right-mindedness in Starbuck, the invulnerable jollity of indifference and recklessness in Stubb, and the pervading mediocrity in Flask. Such a crew, so officered, seemed specially picked and packed by some infernal fatality to help him to his monomaniac revenge. How it was that they so aboundingly responded to the old man's ire—by what evil magic their souls were possessed; the White Whale as much their insufferable foe as his; how he might have seemed the gliding great demon of the seas of life,—all this to explain, would be to dive deeper than Ishmael can go. For one, I gave myself up to the abandonment of the time and the place; but while yet all a-rush to encounter the whale, could see naught in that brute but the deadliest ill.

*I*shmael is clearly not the only one, during this long, appalling day, whose soul is touched by dread. Poor Starbuck, as the pagans drink the savage toast, turns pale, the ship wallows for a strange, long moment as even the wind falters, and from the hold comes a laugh, unexplained, but like an evil omen. — With Ahab gone below, the crew gets wildly drunk, and dances and roars upon the fo'c's'le head. Black Pip is made to play his tambourine, and the mood becomes more violent as a storm begins to rise. Daggoo and a Spanish sailor prepare to fight with fists and knife, but as the seamen — of more than a dozen different lands and races —

C H A P T E R
EIGHT

*Midnight,
Forecastle*

form a ring and cheer for blood,
a squall bursts on the ship. From aft an officer
bellows at the men to shorten sail, and the
drunken violence immediately turns
to sober, violent work as they race to save the ship.

"The squall! the squall," they shout, as they scatter. "Jump, my jollies!" Pip, frightened more by the wildness of the men than by the weather, creeps beneath the windlass as they spring into the rigging to battle with the sails.

"Jollies?" he mutters to himself. "Lord help such jollies! There they go, all cursing, and here I don't. Jimmini, what a squall! But those chaps there are worse yet—they are your white squalls, they. White squalls? white whale! and only this evening that anaconda of an old man swore 'em in to hunt him!"

And he offers up this prayer: "Oh, thou big white God aloft there somewhere in yon darkness, have mercy on this small black boy down here; preserve him from all men that have no bowels to feel fear!"

Later, Pip — who does feel fear, most terribly — goes mad.

The intention of hunting one particular whale, in all the mighty vastness of the globe, is not such a crazy one as it might appear, as Ishmael is at pains to point out in his narrative. There are, indeed, certain seasons for hunting whales in certain places, and the mammals tend to follow specific "veins" along the apparently trackless oceans.

CHAPTER
NINE

The Chart

The sum is, that at particular seasons within that breadth and along that path, migrating whales may with great confidence be looked for. Hence not only at substantiated times, upon well known separate feeding-grounds, could Ahab hope to encounter his prey; but in crossing the widest expanses of water between those grounds he could, by his art, so place and time himself on his way, as even then not to be wholly without prospect of a meeting.

Ishmael also guesses, correctly, that for certain good reasons, Captain Ahab, despite his own desires, will not give up the search for "ordinary" whales. Not only is there potential violence and savagery to be feared if the violent, savage crew were to become bored, but there is also the real, if most unusual, possibility of a kind of "legal mutiny" if Ahab got too lax. If a ship's officers and crew believed their captain had "usurped" the purposes for which the vessel's owners had fitted and provisioned her to go to sea, they could, under maritime law, "refuse all further obedience to him, and even violently wrest from him the command." Ahab, perhaps foolishly, has revealed to them the prime but private purpose of the voyage and, in doing so, has left himself open to this charge.

Be all this as it may, his voice was now often heard hailing the three mast-heads and admonishing them to keep a bright look-out, and not omit reporting even a porpoise. This vigilance was not long without reward.

It was a cloudy, sultry afternoon; the seamen were lazily lounging about the decks, or vacantly gazing over into the lead colored waters. Queequeg and I were mildly employed weaving what is called a sword-mat, for an additional lashing to our boat when I started at a sound so strange, long drawn, and musically wild and unearthly, that the ball of free will dropped from my hand, and I stood gazing up at the clouds whence that voice dropped like a wing. High aloft in the cross-trees was that mad Gay-Header, Tashtego. "There she blows! there! there! there! she blows! she blows!"

"Where-away?" "On the lee-beam, about two miles off! a school of them!" Instantly all was commotion.

The Sperm Whale blows as a clock ticks, with the same undeviating
and reliable uniformity. And thereby whalemen distinguish
this fish from other tribes of his genus.
"There go flukes!" was now the cry from Tashtego;
and the whales disappeared.
"Quick, steward!" cried Ahab. "Time! time!"
Dough-Boy hurried below, glanced at the watch,
and reported the exact minute to Ahab.
The ship was now kept away from the wind, and she went gently rolling
before it. Tashtego reporting that the whales had gone down heading
to leeward, we confidently looked to see them again directly in
advance of our bows. One of the men selected for shipkeepers—
that is, those not appointed to the boats, by this time relieved
the Indian at the main-mast head. The sailors at the fore
and mizzen had come down; the line tubs were fixed in

their places; the cranes were thrust out; the mainyard was backed, and the three boats swung over the sea like three samphire baskets over high cliffs. Outside of the bulwarks their eager crews with one hand clung to the rail, while one foot was expectantly poised on the gunwale.

But at this critical instant a sudden exclamation was heard that took every eye from the whale. With a start all glared at dark Ahab, who was surrounded by five dusky phantoms that seemed fresh formed out of air.

The astonishment of the *Pequod*'s crew at the sight of these men, sprung from nowhere, can scarcely be imagined — but for Ishmael, it is a mystery solved. The shadows on the dockside in Nantucket, Elijah's words, the laughter from the deepest hold. Ahab, it now appears, brought on board, and hid, an extra team of oarsmen. Their leader's name is Fedallah, though some call him the Parsee. Very soon, this strange man from the East forms a weird alliance with Ahab. Fedallah is his captain's prophet, and his Fate. . . .

*T*he Phantoms, for so they then seemed, were flitting on the other side of the deck, and, with a noiseless celerity, were casting loose the tackles and bands of the boat which swung there. This boat had always been deemed one of the spare boats, though technically called the captain's, on account of its hanging from the starboard quarter. The figure that now stood by its bows was tall and swart, with one white tooth evilly protruding from its steel-like lips. A rumpled Chinese jacket of black cotton funereally invested him, with wide black trowsers of the same dark stuff. But strangely crowning this ebonness was a glistening white plaited turban, the living hair braided and coiled round and round upon his head. Less swart in aspect, the companions of this figure were of that vivid, tiger-yellow complexion peculiar to some of the aboriginal natives of the Manillas;—a race notorious for a certain diabolism of subtilty, and by some honest white mariners supposed to be the paid spies and secret confidential agents on the water of the devil, their lord, whose counting-room they suppose to be elsewhere.

CHAPTER
TEN

*The First
Lowering*

While yet the wondering ship's company were gazing upon these strangers, Ahab cried out to the white-turbaned old man at their head,

"All ready there, Fedallah?"

"Ready," was the half-hissed reply.

"Lower away then; d'ye hear?" shouting across the deck.

"Lower away there, I say."

Such was the thunder
of his voice, that spite of
their amazement the men sprang
over the rail; the sheaves whirled round in the
blocks; with a wallow, the three boats dropped into
the sea; while, with a dexterous, off-handed daring,
unknown in any other vocation, the sailors, goat-like,
leaped down the rolling ship's side into the tossed boats below.

Hardly had they pulled out from under the ship's lee, when a fourth keel, coming from the windward side, pulled round under the stern, and showed the five strangers rowing Ahab, who, standing erect in the stern, loudly hailed Starbuck, Stubb, and Flask, to spread themselves widely, so as to cover a large expanse of water. But with all their eyes again riveted upon the swart Fedallah and his crew, the inmates of the other boats obeyed not the command.

"Captain Ahab?—" said Starbuck.

"Spread yourselves," cried Ahab; "give way, all four boats. Thou, Flask, pull out more to leeward!"

"Aye, aye, sir," cheerily cried little King-Post, sweeping round his great steering oar. "Lay back!" addressing his crew. "There!—there!—again! There she blows right ahead, boys!—lay back!"

Now the advent of these outlandish strangers at such a critical instant as the lowering of the boats from the deck, this had not unreasonably awakened a sort of superstitious amazement in some of the ship's company. For me, I silently recalled the mysterious shadows I had seen creeping on board the Pequod during the dim Nantucket dawn, as well as the enigmatical hintings of the unaccountable Elijah.

Meantime, Ahab, out of hearing of his officers, having sided the furthest to windward, was still ranging ahead of the other boats; a circumstance bespeaking how potent a crew was pulling him. Those tiger-yellow creatures of his seemed all steel and whalebone; like five trip-hammers they rose and fell

with regular strokes of strength, which periodically started the boat along the water like a horizontal burst boiler out of a Mississippi steamer. As for Fedallah, who was seen pulling the harpooneer oar, he had thrown aside his black jacket, and displayed his naked chest; while at the other end of the boat Ahab, with one arm, like a fencer's, thrown half backward into the air, was seen steadily managing his steering oar as in a thousand boat lowerings ere the White Whale had torn him. All at once the outstretched arm gave a peculiar motion and then remained fixed, while the boat's five oars were seen simultaneously peaked. Boat and crew sat motionless on the sea. Instantly the three spread boats in the rear paused on their way. The whales had irregularly settled bodily down into the blue, thus giving no distantly discernible token of the movement, though from his closer vicinity Ahab had observed it.

"Every man look out along his oar!" cried Starbuck. "Thou, Queequeg, stand up!"

Not very far distant Flask's boat was also lying breathlessly still; its commander recklessly standing upon the top of the loggerhead, a stout sort of post rooted in the keel, and rising some two feet above the level of the stern platform. But little King-Post was small and short, and at the same time little King-Post was full of a large and tall ambition, so that this loggerhead standpoint of his did by no means satisfy King-Post.

"I can't see three seas off; tip us up an oar there, and let me on to that."

Upon this, Daggoo, with either hand upon the gunwale to steady his way, swiftly slid aft, and then erecting himself volunteered his lofty shoulders for a pedestal.

"Good a mast-head as any, sir. Will you mount?"

"That I will, and thank ye very much, my fine fellow; only I wish you fifty feet taller."

Whereupon planting his feet firmly against two opposite planks of the boat, the gigantic negro, stooping a little, presented his flat palm to Flask's foot, and then putting Flask's hand on his hearse-plumed head and bidding him spring as he himself should toss, with one dexterous fling landed the little man high and dry on his shoulders. And here was Flask now standing, Daggoo with one lifted arm furnishing him with a breast-band to lean against and steady himself by. At any time it is a strange sight to the tyro to see with what wondrous habitude of unconscious skill the whale man will maintain an erect posture in his boat, even when pitched about by the most riotously perverse and cross-running seas. Still more strange to see him giddily perched upon the loggerhead itself, under such circumstances. But the sight of little Flask mounted upon gigantic Daggoo was yet more curious; for sustaining himself with a cool, indifferent, easy, unthought of, barbaric majesty, the noble negro to every roll of the sea harmoniously rolled his fine form. On his broad back, flaxen-haired Flask seemed a snow-flake. The bearer looked nobler than the rider. Though, truly, vivacious, tumultuous, ostentatious little Flask would now and then stamp with impatience; but not one added heave did he thereby give to the negro's lordly chest.

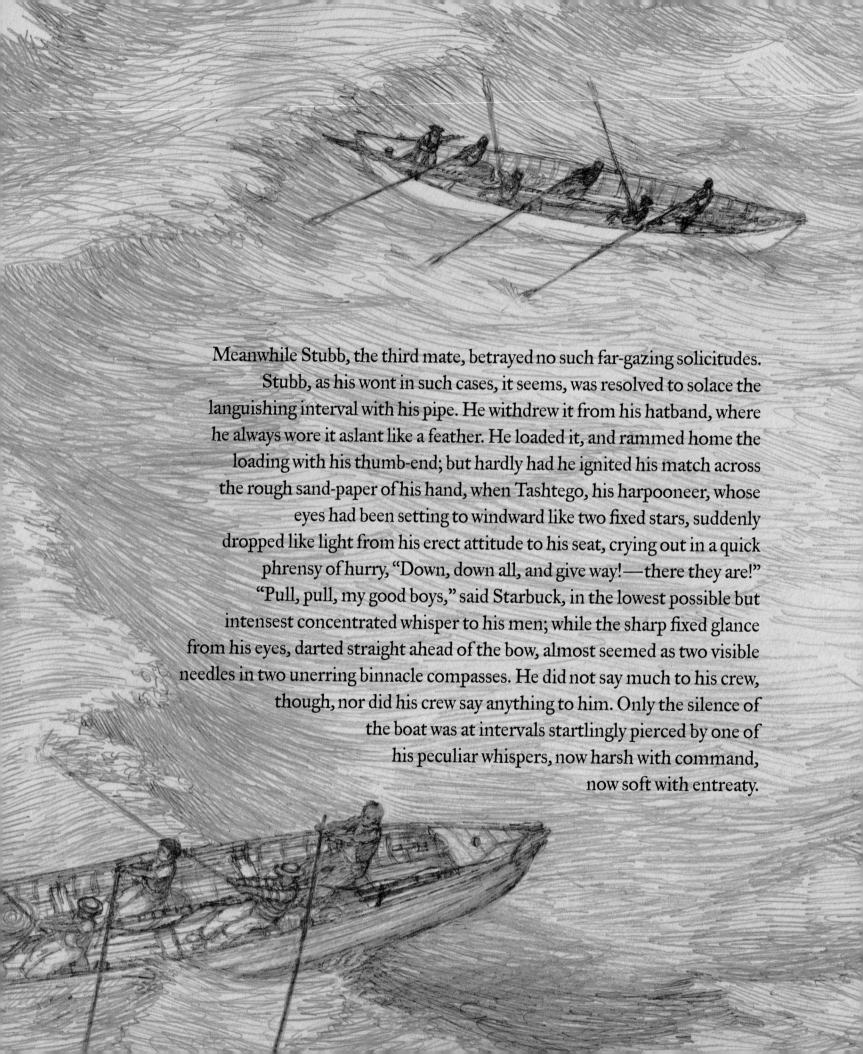

Meanwhile Stubb, the third mate, betrayed no such far-gazing solicitudes. Stubb, as his wont in such cases, it seems, was resolved to solace the languishing interval with his pipe. He withdrew it from his hatband, where he always wore it aslant like a feather. He loaded it, and rammed home the loading with his thumb-end; but hardly had he ignited his match across the rough sand-paper of his hand, when Tashtego, his harpooneer, whose eyes had been setting to windward like two fixed stars, suddenly dropped like light from his erect attitude to his seat, crying out in a quick phrensy of hurry, "Down, down all, and give way!—there they are!"

"Pull, pull, my good boys," said Starbuck, in the lowest possible but intensest concentrated whisper to his men; while the sharp fixed glance from his eyes, darted straight ahead of the bow, almost seemed as two visible needles in two unerring binnacle compasses. He did not say much to his crew, though, nor did his crew say anything to him. Only the silence of the boat was at intervals startlingly pierced by one of his peculiar whispers, now harsh with command, now soft with entreaty.

How different the loud little King-Post. "Sing out and say something, my hearties. Roar and pull, my thunderbolts! Beach me, beach me on their black backs, boys; only do that for me, and I'll sign over to you my Martha's Vineyard plantation, boys; including wife and children, boys. Lay me on—lay me on! O Lord, Lord! but I shall go stark, staring mad: See! see that white water!" And so shouting, he pulled his hat from his head, and stamped up and down on it; then picking it up, flirted it far off upon the sea; and finally fell to rearing and plunging in the boat's stern like a crazed colt from the prairie.

"Look at that chap now," philosophically drawled Stubb, who, with his unlighted short pipe, mechanically retained between his teeth, followed after—"He's got fits, that Flask has. Fits? yes, give him fits—that's the very word—pitch fits into 'em. Merrily, merrily, hearts-alive. Pudding for supper, you know;—merry's the word. Only pull, and keep pulling; nothing more. Crack all your backbones and bite your knives in two—that's all. Take it easy—why don't ye take it easy, I say, and burst all your livers and lungs!"

But what it was that inscrutable Ahab said to that tiger-yellow crew of his—these were words best omitted here; for you live under the blessed light of the evangelical land. Only the infidel sharks in the audacious seas may give ear to such words, when, with tornado brow, and eyes of red murder, and foam-glued lips, Ahab leaped after his prey. Meanwhile, all the boats tore on. It was a sight full of quick wonder and awe!

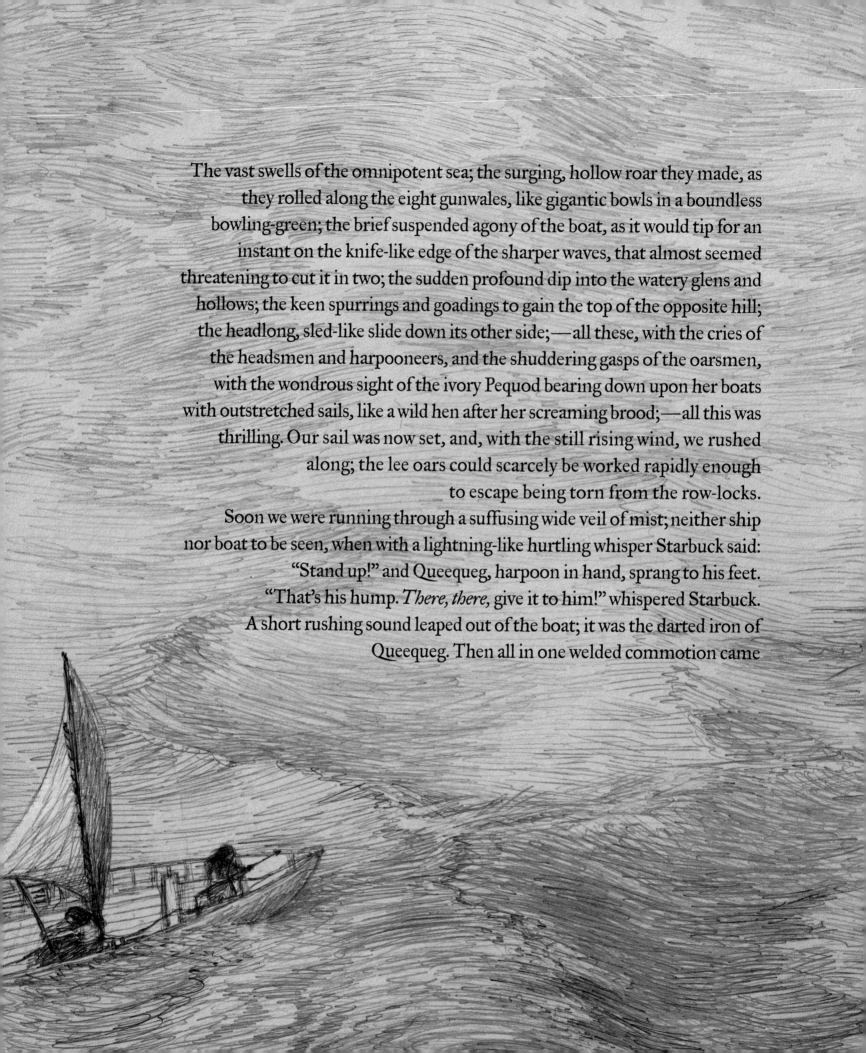

The vast swells of the omnipotent sea; the surging, hollow roar they made, as
they rolled along the eight gunwales, like gigantic bowls in a boundless
bowling-green; the brief suspended agony of the boat, as it would tip for an
instant on the knife-like edge of the sharper waves, that almost seemed
threatening to cut it in two; the sudden profound dip into the watery glens and
hollows; the keen spurrings and goadings to gain the top of the opposite hill;
the headlong, sled-like slide down its other side;—all these, with the cries of
the headsmen and harpooneers, and the shuddering gasps of the oarsmen,
with the wondrous sight of the ivory Pequod bearing down upon her boats
with outstretched sails, like a wild hen after her screaming brood;—all this was
thrilling. Our sail was now set, and, with the still rising wind, we rushed
along; the lee oars could scarcely be worked rapidly enough
to escape being torn from the row-locks.
Soon we were running through a suffusing wide veil of mist; neither ship
nor boat to be seen, when with a lightning-like hurtling whisper Starbuck said:
"Stand up!" and Queequeg, harpoon in hand, sprang to his feet.
"That's his hump. *There, there,* give it to him!" whispered Starbuck.
A short rushing sound leaped out of the boat; it was the darted iron of
Queequeg. Then all in one welded commotion came

an invisible push from astern, while forward the boat seemed striking on a ledge; the sail collapsed and exploded; a gush of scalding vapor shot up near by; something rolled and tumbled like an earthquake beneath us. The whole crew were half suffocated as they were tossed helter-skelter into the white curdling cream of the squall. Squall, whale, and harpoon had all blended together; and the whale, merely grazed by the iron, escaped.

Though completely swamped, the boat was nearly unharmed. Swimming round it we picked up the floating oars, and lashing them across the gunwale, tumbled back to our places. There we sat up to our knees in the sea, the water covering every rib and plank, so that to our downward gazing eyes the suspended craft seemed a coral boat grown up to us from the bottom of the ocean.

The wind increased to a howl; the waves dashed their bucklers together; the whole squall roared, forked, and crackled around us like a white fire upon the prairie, in which, unconsumed, we were burning; immortal in these jaws of death! In vain we hailed the other boats; as well roar to the live coals down the chimney of a flaming furnace as hail those boats in that storm. Meanwhile the driving scud, rack, and mist, grew darker with the shadows of night; no sign of the ship could be seen. The rising sea forbade all attempts to bale out the boat. The oars were useless as propellers, performing now the office of life-preservers. So, cutting the lashing of the waterproof match keg, after many failures Starbuck contrived to ignite the lamp in the lantern; then stretching it on a waif-pole, handed it to Queequeg as the standard-bearer of this forlorn hope. There, then, he sat, holding up that imbecile candle in the heart of that almighty forlornness. There, then, he sat, the sign and symbol of a man without faith, hopelessly holding up hope in the midst of despair.

Wet, drenched through, and shivering cold, despairing of ship or boat, we lifted up our eyes as the dawn came on. The mist still spread over the sea, the empty lantern lay crushed in the bottom of the boat. Suddenly Queequeg started to his feet, hollowing his hand to his ear. We all heard a faint creaking, as of ropes and yards hitherto muffled by the storm. The sound came nearer and nearer; the thick mists were dimly parted by a huge, vague form. Affrighted, we all sprang into the sea as the ship at last loomed into view, bearing right down upon us within a distance of not much more than its length.

Floating on the waves we saw the abandoned boat, as for one instant it tossed and gaped beneath the ship's bows like a chip at the base of a cataract; and then the vast hull rolled over it, and it was seen no more till it came up weltering astern. Again we swam for it, were dashed against it by the seas, and were at last taken up and safely landed on board. Ere the squall came close to, the other

boats had cut loose from their fish and returned to the ship in good time. The ship had given us up, but was still cruising, if haply it might light upon some token of our perishing,—an oar or a lance pole.

"Queequeg," said I, when they had dragged me, the last man, to the deck, and I was still shaking myself in my jacket to fling off the water; "Queequeg, my fine friend, does this sort of thing often happen?" Without much emotion, though soaked through just like me, he gave me to understand that such things did often happen.

"Mr. Stubb," said I, turning to that worthy, who, buttoned up in his oil-jacket, was now calmly smoking his pipe in the rain; "Mr. Stubb, I think I have heard you say that of all whalemen you ever met, our chief mate, Mr. Starbuck, is by far the most careful and prudent. I suppose then, that going plump on a flying whale with your sail set in a foggy squall is the height of a whaleman's discretion?"

"Certain. I've lowered for whales from a leaking ship in a gale off Cape Horn."

"Mr. Flask," said I, turning to little King-Post, who was standing close by; "you are experienced in these things, and I am not. Will you tell me whether it is an unalterable law in this fishery, Mr. Flask, for an oarsman to break his own back pulling himself back-foremost into death's jaws?"

"Yes, that's the law. I should like to see a boat's crew backing water up to a whale face foremost. Ha, ha! the whale would give them squint for squint, mind that!"

Here then, from three impartial witnesses, I had a deliberate statement of the entire case. And considering in what a devil's chase I was implicated, touching the White Whale: I thought I might as well go below and make a rough draft of my will.

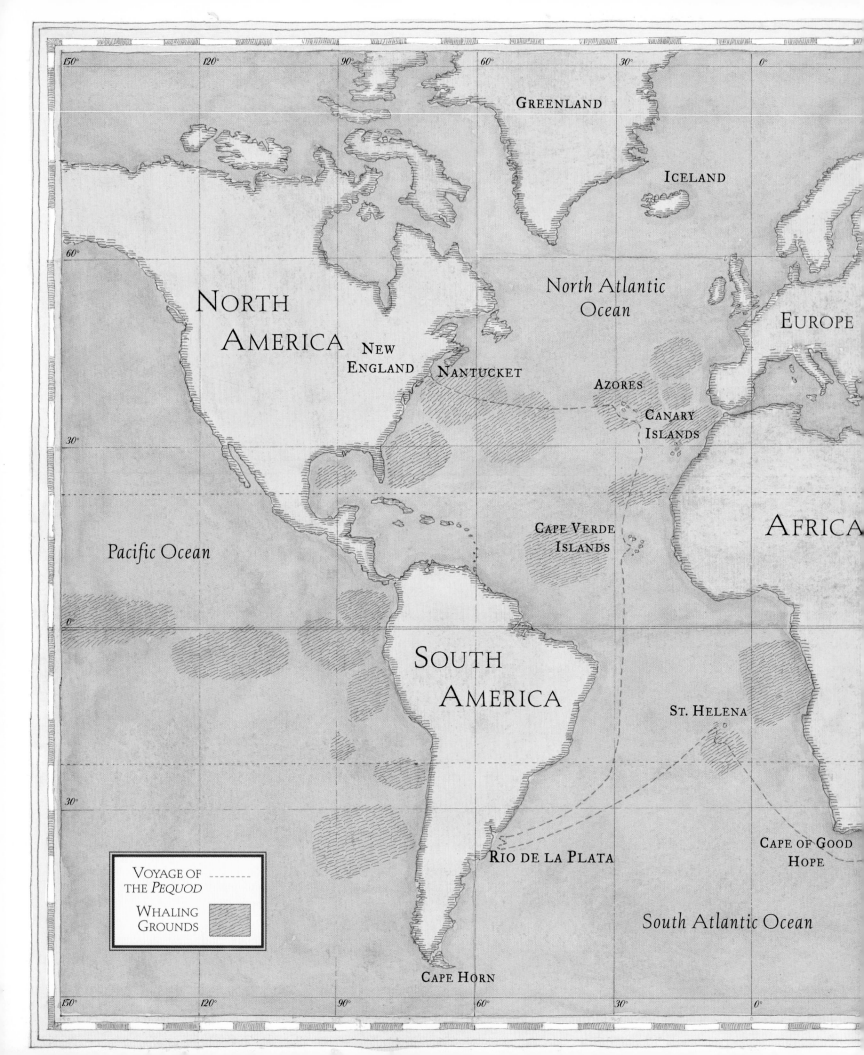

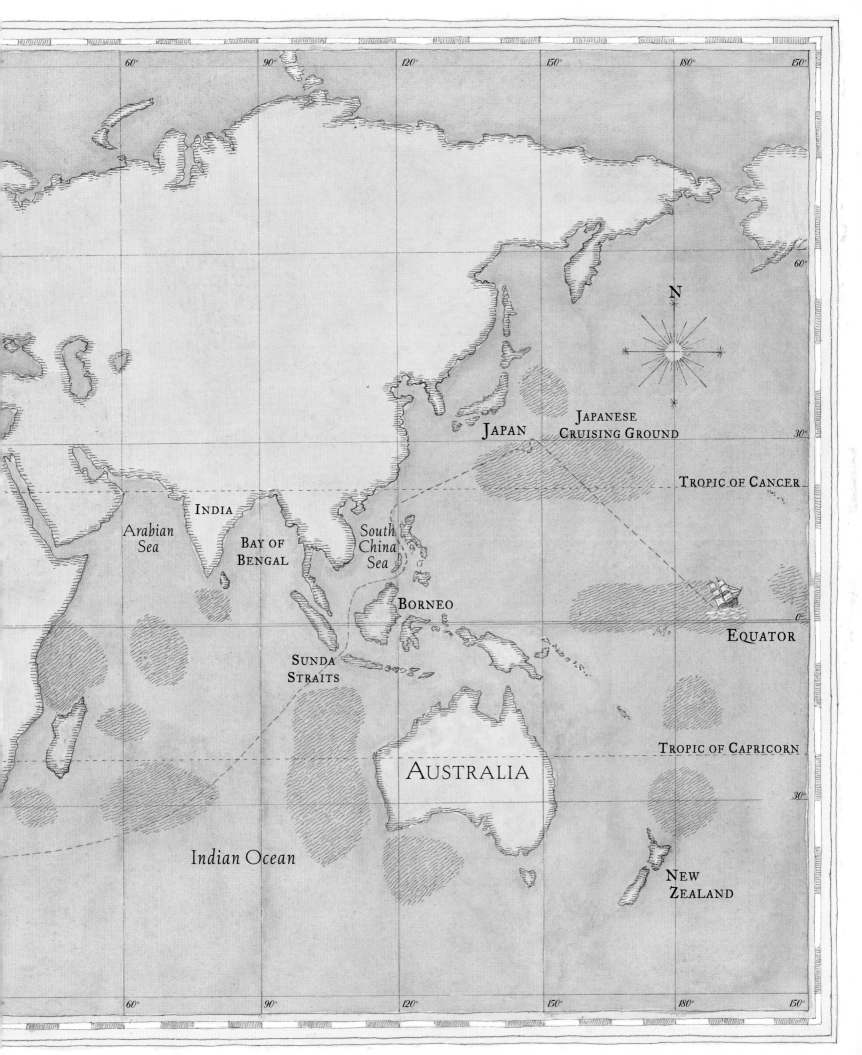

Days, weeks passed, and under easy sail, the ivory Pequod had slowly swept across four several cruising-grounds; that off the Azores; off the Cape de Verdes; on the Plate (so called), being off the mouth of the Rio de la Plata; and the Carrol Ground, an unstaked, watery locality, southerly from St. Helena.

CHAPTER ELEVEN

The Spirit-Spout

It was while gliding through these latter waters that one serene and moonlight night, when all the waves rolled by like scrolls of silver: on such a silent night a silvery jet was seen far in advance of the white bubbles at the bow. Lit up by the moon, it looked celestial; seemed some plumed and glittering god uprising from the sea. Fedallah first descried this jet. For of these moonlight nights, it was his wont to mount to the main-mast head, and stand a look-out there, with the same precision as if it had been day. And yet, though herds of whales were seen by night, not one whaleman in a hundred would venture a lowering for them.

"There she blows!"

Had the trump of judgment blown, they could not have quivered more; yet still they felt no terror; rather pleasure. For though it was a most unwonted hour, yet so impressive was the cry, and so deliriously exciting, that almost every soul on board instinctively desired a lowering.

Walking the deck with quick, side-lunging strides, Ahab commanded the t'gallant sails and royals to be set, and every stunsail spread. The best man in the ship must take the helm. Then, with every mast-head manned, the piled-up craft rolled down before the wind. The strange, upheaving, lifting tendency of the taffrail breeze filling the hollows of so many sails, made the buoyant, hovering deck to feel like air beneath the feet; while still she rushed along, as if two antagonistic influences were struggling in her—one to mount direct to heaven, the other to drive yawingly to some horizontal goal. But though the ship so swiftly sped, and though from every eye, like arrows, the eager glances shot, yet the silvery jet was no more seen that night. Every sailor swore he saw it once, but not a second time.

This midnight-spout had almost grown a forgotten thing, when, some days after, lo! at the same silent hour, it was again announced: again it was descried by all; but upon making sail to overtake it, once more it disappeared as if it had never been. And so it served us night after night, till no one heeded it but to wonder at it. Mysteriously jetted into the clear moonlight, or starlight, as the case might be; disappearing again for one whole day, or two days, or three; and somehow seeming at every distinct repetition to be advancing still further and further in our van, this solitary jet seemed for ever alluring us on.

Nor with the immemorial superstition of their race, and in accordance with the preternaturalness, as it seemed, which in many things invested the Pequod, were there wanting some of the seamen who swore that whenever and wherever descried; at however remote times, or in however far apart latitudes and longitudes, that unnearable spout was cast by one self-same whale; and that whale, Moby Dick. For a time, there reigned, too, a sense of peculiar dread at this flitting apparition, as if it were treacherously beckoning us on and on, in order that the monster might turn round upon us, and rend us at last in the remotest and most savage seas.

But, at last, when turning to the eastward, the Cape winds began howling around us, and we rose and fell upon the long, troubled seas that are there; when the ivory-tusked Pequod sharply bowed to the blast, and gored the dark waves in her madness; then all this desolate vacuity of life went away, but gave place to sights more dismal than before.

Close to our bows, strange forms in the water darted hither and thither before us; while thick in our rear flew the inscrutable sea-ravens. And every morning, perched on our stays, rows of these birds were seen, as though they deemed our ship some drifting, uninhabited craft; a thing appointed to desolation, and therefore fit roosting-place for their homeless selves.

Cape of Good Hope, do they call ye? Rather Cape Tormentoso, as called of yore; for we found ourselves launched into this tormented sea, where guilty beings transformed into those fowls and these fish, seemed condemned to swim on everlastingly without any haven in store, or beat that black air without any horizon. But calm, snow-white, and unvarying; still directing its fountain of feathers to the sky; still beckoning us on from before, the solitary jet would at times be descried.

South-eastward from the Cape, off the distant Crozetts, a sail loomed ahead, the Goney (Albatross) by name. As she slowly drew nigh, from my lofty perch at the fore-mast-head, I had a good view of that sight so remarkable to a tyro in the far ocean fisheries—a whaler at sea, and long absent from home.

CHAPTER TWELVE

The Albatross

As if the waves had been fullers, this craft was bleached like the skeleton of a stranded walrus. All down her sides, this spectral appearance was traced with long channels of reddened rust, while all her spars and her rigging were like the thick branches of trees furred over with hoar-frost. Only her lower sails were set. A wild sight it was to see her long-bearded look-outs at those three mast-heads. They seemed clad in the skins of beasts, so torn and bepatched the raiment that had survived nearly four years of cruising. Standing in iron hoops nailed to the mast, they swayed and swung over a fathomless sea; and though, when the ship slowly glided close under our stern, we six men in the air came so nigh to each other that we might almost have leaped from the mast-heads of one ship to those of the other; yet, those forlorn-looking fishermen, mildly eyeing us as they passed, said not one word to our own look-outs, while the quarter-deck hail was being heard from below.

"Ship ahoy! Have ye seen the White Whale?"

But as the strange captain, leaning over the pallid bulwarks, was in the act of putting his trumpet to his mouth, it somehow fell from his hand into the sea; and the wind now rising amain, he in vain strove to make himself heard without it. Ahab for a moment paused; it almost seemed as though he would have lowered a boat to board the stranger, had not the threatening wind forbade. But taking advantage of his windward position, he again seized his trumpet, and knowing by her aspect that the stranger vessel was a Nantucketer and shortly bound home, he loudly hailed—"Ahoy there! This is the Pequod, bound round the world! Tell them to address all future letters to the Pacific ocean! and this time three years, if I am not at home, tell them to address them to—"

At that moment the two wakes were fairly crossed, and instantly, then, in accordance with their singular ways, shoals of small harmless fish, that for some days before had been placidly swimming by our side, darted away with what seemed shuddering fins, and ranged themselves fore and aft with the stranger's flanks. Though in the course of his continual voyagings Ahab must often before have noticed a similar sight, yet, to any monomaniac man, the veriest trifles capriciously carry meanings.

"Swim away from me, do ye?" murmured Ahab, gazing over into the water. There seemed but little in the words, but the tone conveyed more of deep helpless sadness than the insane old man had ever before evinced. But turning to the steersman, who thus far had been holding the ship in the wind to diminish her headway, he cried out in his old lion voice,—"Up helm! Keep her off round the world!"

Round the world!

After the Cape of Good Hope (which was formerly called the Cape of Storms, and possibly Tormentoso, as Ishmael insists) the *Pequod* heads across the Indian Ocean. The next ship they meet is named the *Town-Ho*, crewed almost entirely by Polynesian islanders and, like the *Albatross*, returning to America. With this ship, the *Pequod* has a "gam." ⁓ This, according to Ishmael, is "a thing so utterly unknown to all other ships that they never heard of the name even; and if by chance they should hear of it, they only grin at it, and repeat gamesome stuff about 'spouters' and 'blubber-boilers,' and such like pretty exclamations." It is a word, he insists, that is not in any dictionary, so he gives his own "learned" definition: **GAM. Noun — A social meeting of two [or more] Whale-ships, generally on a cruising-ground; when, after exchanging hails, they exchange visits by boats' crews: the two captains remaining, for the time, on board one ship, and the two chief mates on the other.** ⁓ During the *Town-Ho* gam, some sailors on the *Pequod* hear a story of the white whale. The story has elements of such significance, however, that they agree it is better kept from Ahab: a violent, bitter officer is killed deliberately in the monster's jaws. And the *Pequod* sets sail once more, northeastward in a serene and languid breeze toward Java, still guided, haunted, "at wide intervals in the silvery night," by the "lonely, alluring" spirit-spout. ⁓ Ishmael, feeling philosophical, muses on the difference between the sea —"a foe to man, a fiend to its own offspring"— and the "green, gentle, and most docile earth." The sea is subtle, hiding its most dreaded specimens "beneath the loveliest tints of azure," where all its creatures "prey upon each other, carrying on eternal war since the world began," and he warns mankind to beware its "universal cannibalism."

CHAPTER
THIRTEEN

The Gam

There is no doubt that Ishmael sees all of us adrift in the "appalling ocean" that is life.
⟶ As if to illustrate the dangers and the mysteries we must face, the *Pequod* still in
lovely waters, spots its prey at last. Daggoo's masthead cry rouses every man onboard
to great excitement.

"There! there again! there she breaches! right ahead! The White Whale, the
White Whale!"

⟶ But it very quickly becomes apparent it is not. This time the ocean, full of treachery, has
thrown up a creature that fills the superstitious whalemen with a mythic dread. The four boats, as
they approach, see a "white mass" in the water, which mysteriously submerges, then slowly
rises once again. Ishmael, with the others, is overawed.

Almost forgetting for the moment all thoughts of Moby Dick, we now
gazed at the most wondrous phenomenon which the secret seas have hitherto
revealed to mankind. A vast pulpy mass, furlongs in length and breadth, of a
glancing cream-color, lay floating on the water, innumerable long arms
radiating from its centre, and curling and twisting like a nest of anacondas, as
if blindly to clutch at any hapless object within reach. No perceptible face or
front did it have; no conceivable token of either sensation or instinct; but
undulated there on the billows, an unearthly, formless, chance-like apparition
of life.

As with a low sucking sound it slowly disappeared again, Starbuck with a wild
voice exclaimed—"Almost rather had I seen Moby Dick and fought him, than
to have seen thee, thou white ghost!"

"What was it, Sir?" said Flask.

"The great live squid, which, they say, few whale-ships ever beheld, and
returned to their ports to tell of it."

But Ahab said nothing; turning his boat, he sailed back to the vessel; the rest
as silently following. ⚭

*T*he next day was exceedingly still and sultry, and with nothing special to engage them, the Pequod's crew could hardly resist the spell of sleep induced by such a vacant sea. It was my turn to stand at the foremast-head; and with my shoulders leaning against the slackened royal shrouds, to and fro I idly swayed in what seemed an enchanted air.

Suddenly bubbles seemed bursting beneath my closed eyes; like vices my hands grasped the shrouds; some invisible, gracious agency preserved me; with a shock I came back to life. And lo! close under our lee, not forty fathoms off, a gigantic Sperm Whale lay rolling in the water like the capsized hull of a frigate, his broad, glossy back glistening in the sun's rays like a mirror. As if struck by some enchanter's wand, the sleepy ship and every sleeper in it all at once started into wakefulness; and more than a score of voices shouted forth the accustomed cry.

The sudden exclamations of the crew must have alarmed the whale; and ere the boats were down, majestically turning, he swam away to the leeward.

CHAPTER
FOURTEEN

*Stubb
Kills a Whale*

"There go flukes!" was the cry, an announcement immediately followed by Stubb's producing his match and igniting his pipe, for now a respite was granted. After the full interval of his sounding had elapsed, the whale rose again, and Stubb counted upon the honor of the capture.

"Start her, start her, my men! Don't hurry yourselves; take plenty of time—but start her; start her like thunder-claps, that's all. Start her like grim death and grinning devils, and raise the buried dead perpendicular out of their graves, boys— that's all. Start her!"

Like desperadoes they tugged and they strained, till the welcome cry was heard—"Stand up, Tashtego!—give it to him!" The harpoon was hurled. "Stern all!" The oarsmen backed water; the same moment something went hot and hissing along every one of their wrists. It was the magical line. An instant before, Stubb had swiftly caught two additional turns with it round the loggerhead, whence, by reason of its increased rapid circlings, a hempen blue smoke now jetted up and mingled with the steady fumes from his pipe.

"Haul in—haul in!" cried Stubb to the bowsman; and, facing round towards the whale, all hands began pulling the boat up to him, while yet the boat was being towed on. Soon ranging up by his flank, Stubb, firmly planting his knee in the clumsy cleat, darted dart after dart into the flying fish; at the word of command, the boat alternately sterning out of the way of the whale's horrible wallow, and then ranging up for another fling.

"Pull up—pull up!" he now cried to the bowsman, as the waning whale relaxed in his wrath. "Pull up!—close to!" and the boat ranged along the fish's flank. When reaching far over the bow, Stubb slowly churned his long sharp lance into the fish, and kept it there, carefully churning and churning, as if cautiously seeking to feel after some gold watch that the whale might have swallowed, and which he was fearful of breaking ere he could hook it out. But that gold watch he sought was the innermost life of the fish. And now it is struck; for, starting from his trance into that unspeakable thing called his "flurry," the monster horribly wallowed in his blood, overwrapped himself in impenetrable, mad, boiling spray, so that the imperilled craft, instantly dropping astern, had much ado blindly to struggle out from that phrensied twilight into the clear air of the day.

And now abating in his flurry, the whale once more rolled out into view; surging from side to side; spasmodically dilating and contracting his spout-hole, with sharp, cracking, agonized respirations. At last, gush after gush of clotted red gore, as if it had been the purple lees of red wine, shot into the frightened air; and falling back again, ran dripping down his motionless flanks into the sea. His heart had burst!

"He's dead, Mr. Stubb," said Tashtego.

"Yes; both pipes smoked out!" and withdrawing his own from his mouth, Stubb scattered the dead ashes over the water; and, for a moment, stood thoughtfully eyeing the vast corpse he had made.

Stubb's whale had been killed some distance from the ship. It was a calm; so, forming a tandem of three boats, we commenced the slow business of towing the trophy to the Pequod. Darkness came on; but three lights up and down in the main-rigging dimly guided our way; till drawing nearer we saw Ahab dropping one of several more lanterns over the bulwarks. Vacantly eyeing the heaving whale for a moment, he issued the usual orders for securing it for the night, and then handing his lantern to a seaman, went his way into the cabin, and did not come forward again until morning.

If moody Ahab was now all quiescence, Stubb, his second mate, flushed with conquest, betrayed an unusual but still good-natured excitement. Stubb was a high liver; he was somewhat intemperately fond of the whale as a flavorish thing to his palate.

"A steak, a steak, ere I sleep! You, Daggoo! overboard you go, and cut me one!"

About midnight that steak was cut and cooked; and lighted by two lanterns of sperm oil, Stubb stoutly stood up to his spermaceti supper at the capstan-head, as if that capstan were a sideboard. Nor was Stubb the only banqueter on whale's flesh that night. Mingling their mumblings with his own mastications, thousands on thousands of sharks, swarming round the dead leviathan, smackingly feasted on its fatness. A shocking sharkish business enough for all parties; and though sharks also are the invariable outriders of all slave ships crossing the Atlantic, systematically trotting alongside, to be handy in case a parcel is to be carried anywhere, or a dead slave to be decently buried; yet is there no conceivable time or occasion when you will find them in such countless numbers, and in gayer or more jovial spirits, than around a dead sperm whale, moored by night to a whale-ship at sea.

It was a Saturday night, and such a Sabbath as followed! Ex officio professors of Sabbath breaking are all whalemen. The ivory Pequod was turned into what seemed a shamble; every sailor a butcher. You would have thought we were offering up ten thousand red oxen to the sea gods.

CHAPTER
FIFTEEN

Cutting In

In the first place, the enormous cutting tackles were swayed up to the main-top and firmly lashed to the lower mast-head, the strongest point anywhere above a ship's deck. The end of the rope was then conducted to the windlass, and the huge lower block of the tackles was swung over the whale; to this block the great blubber hook was attached. And now suspended in stages over the side, Starbuck and Stubb, armed with their long spades, began cutting a hole in the body for the insertion of the hook just above the nearest of the two side-fins. This done, the main body of the crew now commence heaving in one dense crowd at the windlass. When instantly, the entire ship careens over on her side; she trembles, quivers, and nods her frighted mast-heads to the sky. More and more she leans over; till at last, a swift, startling snap is heard; with a great swash the ship rolls upwards and backwards from the whale, and the triumphant tackle rises into sight dragging after it the first strip of blubber. Now as the blubber envelops the whale precisely as the rind does an orange, so is it stripped off from the body precisely as an orange is sometimes stripped by spiralizing it. For the strain constantly kept up by the windlass continually keeps the whale rolling over and over in the water; and just as fast as it is thus peeled off, it is all the time being hoisted higher and higher aloft till its upper end grazes the main-top.

One of the attending harpooneers now advances with a long, keen weapon called a boarding-sword, and dexterously slices out a considerable hole in the lower part of the swaying mass. Into this hole, the end of the second alternating great tackle is then hooked. Whereupon, this accomplished swordsman severs it completely; so that the long upper strip swings clear, all ready for lowering. And thus the work proceeds; the two tackles hoisting and lowering simultaneously; both whale and windlass heaving, the heavers singing, the blubber-room gentlemen coiling, the ship straining, and all hands swearing occasionally, by way of assuaging the general friction.

The Pequod's whale being decapitated and the body stripped, the head was hoisted against the ship's side—about half way out of the sea, so that it might yet in great part be buoyed up by its native element. And there with the strained craft steeply leaning over to it, that blood-dripping head hung to the Pequod's waist like the giant Holofernes's from the girdle of Judith.

After this biblical reference (Holofernes is a giant warrior whose head Judith cuts off, clearly a metaphor for whaling to our scholar-seaman), Ishmael explains that Queequeg has to balance on the revolving corpse throughout the whole dangerous operation of stripping the blubber, or "flensing," which leaves him trembling with exhaustion, with "blue lips and bloodshot eyes." He is then handed a drink by the steward, which turns out not to be the traditional hot brandy — but "a cup of ginger and water." Stubb, scandalized, accuses "Mr. Dough-Boy" of trying to poison Queequeg and runs below, to reappear with a flask of fiery spirits. The culprit, it turns out though, is not the steward but Bildad's pious Quaker sister, Aunt Charity, who brought the "ginger-jub" onboard before they left Nantucket and insisted he should serve it to the harpooneers to save them from the evils of strong drink. Charity's kind gift, however, is "freely given to the waves" — Stubb throws it overboard. Honor — and Queequeg — are satisfied.

Ishmael then goes on to describe an operation even more appallingly dangerous than Queequeg's. The head of the whale, hacked off from the body, is hoisted on tackles to dangle from two great hooks, while the stripped corpse is allowed to drift away and sink or rot. It is Tashtego's job to cut a passageway into the part of the skull called the case, which contains "by far the most precious of all his oily vintages; namely, the highly-prized spermaceti." Then he has to balance himself at the mouth of this slippery, bloody "cistern" and dip out the contents — up to five hundred gallons — with a single bucket. He holds only a thin line for "safety" and toward the end of the process must thrust his bucket twenty-five feet or more into the case with a pole. This time, there is a "queer accident."

CHAPTER SIXTEEN

Cistern and Buckets

How it was exactly, there is no telling now; but, on a sudden, as the eightieth or ninetieth bucket came suckingly up—my God! poor Tashtego—dropped head-foremost, and with a horrible oily gurgling, went clean out of sight!

"Man overboard!" cried Daggoo, who amid the general consternation first came to his senses. Looking over the side, they saw the before lifeless head throbbing and heaving just below the surface of the sea, as if that moment seized with some momentous idea; whereas it was only the poor Indian unconsciously revealing by those struggles the perilous depth to which he had sunk.

At this instant, a sharp cracking noise was heard; and to the unspeakable horror of all, one of the two enormous hooks suspending the head tore out, and with a vast vibration the enormous mass sideways swung, till the drunk ship reeled and shook as if smitten by an iceberg.

"Stand clear of the tackle!" cried a voice like the bursting of a rocket.

Almost in the same instant, with a thunder-boom, the enormous mass dropped into the sea; the suddenly relieved hull rolled away from it, while poor, buried-alive Tashtego was sinking utterly down to the bottom of the sea! But hardly had the blinding vapor cleared away, when a naked figure with a boarding-sword in its hand, was for one swift moment seen hovering over the bulwarks. The next, a loud splash announced that my brave Queequeg had dived to the rescue. One packed rush was made to the side, and every eye counted every ripple, as moment followed moment, and no sign of either the sinker or the diver could be seen.

"Ha! ha!" cried Daggoo, all at once; and looking further off from the side, we saw an arm thrust upright from the blue waves; a strange sight to see, as an arm thrust forth from the grass over a grave.

"Both! both!—it is both!"—cried Daggoo again with a joyful shout; and soon after, Queequeg was seen boldly striking out with one hand, and with the other clutching the long hair of the Indian. Diving after the slowly descending head, Queequeg with his keen sword had made side lunges near its bottom, so as to scuttle a large hole there; then dropping his sword, had thrust his long arm far inwards and upwards, and so hauled out our poor Tash by the head. He averred, that upon first thrusting in for him, a leg was presented; but well knowing that that was not as it ought to be, and might occasion great trouble;—he had thrust back the leg, and by a dexterous heave and toss, had wrought a somerset upon the Indian; so that with the next trial, he came forth in the good old way—head foremost. As for the great head itself, that was doing as well as could be expected.

Midwifery should be taught in the same course with fencing and boxing, riding and rowing.

As the *Pequod* ranges slowly across the worldwide whaling grounds, she inevitably meets many other whale ships. Ahab's destiny, as he sees it, is to find and kill the white whale, and each ship, he knows in his heart, has been placed across his pathway to be questioned for the smallest clue. Ishmael, although

appearing to accept this weird philosophy, is skeptical. Some parts of it he treats more like a bitter joke. Frenchmen, Dutchmen, Germans, British — Nantucketers have little admiration or respect for them as whalers. But these "predestinated" meetings, to echo Ishmael's word, are meant to tell us as much about Americans and their attitudes as they are about the cardboard cutout "foreigners" who are so feeble at the game. Consider when they meet the good ship *Jungfrau* (Virgin), out of Bremen, for example; commanded by an incompetent named Derick De Deer. ⌒ The *Virgin*'s men — so completely useless have they been at catching whales — are forced to row up to the *Pequod* when they meet her to beg some oil for their lamps! When spouts are seen, they are much closer to the whales than the *Pequod*'s men, but are overtaken easily and thus lose the only prize to be taken on this day. A good chase, a chance to mock the Germans, terrific seamanship by the brave Americans — all fine heroics, up to a point. Then Ishmael decides to spoil it. The whale is extremely old — indeed, they find a stone lance-head buried in its flesh when they cut into it — and they treat it very barbarously.

CHAPTER
SEVENTEEN

*The Pequod
Meets the
Virgin*

As the boats now more closely surrounded him, the whole upper part of his form, with much of it that is ordinarily submerged, was plainly revealed. His eyes, or rather the places where his eyes had been, were beheld. As strange misgrown masses gather in the knot-holes of the noblest oaks when prostrate,

so from the points which the whale's eyes had once occupied, now protruded blind bulbs, horribly pitiable to see. But pity there was none. For all his old age, he must die the death and be murdered, in order to light the gay bridals and other merry-makings of men, and also to illuminate the solemn churches that preach unconditional inoffensiveness by all to all. Still rolling in his blood, at last he partially disclosed a strangely discolored bunch or protuberance, the size of a bushel, low down on the flank.

"A nice spot," cried Flask; "just let me prick him there once."

"Avast!" cried Starbuck, "there's no need of that!"

But humane Starbuck was too late. At the instant of the dart an ulcerous jet shot from this cruel wound, and goaded by it into more than sufferable anguish, the whale now spouting thick blood, with swift fury blindly darted at the craft, bespattering them and their glorying crews all over with showers of gore, capsizing Flask's boat and marring the bows. It was his death stroke.

The whale's death stroke, maybe — but he has his revenge. Back at the ship, before the whalemen can get far into the process of turning him into cash, the whale begins to sink — and has to be chopped free from the *Pequod* before she is capsized by the sinking weight. On the discovery of the stone lance, Ishmael wondered: "Who had darted that? And when? It might have been darted by some Nor' West Indian long before America was discovered." Philosophy again? Not only are the modern, fine Americans seen as barbarians in some respects, but Ishmael might intend the ancient whale to represent America itself. The white men hunt and cruelly slaughter it, but by very virtue of its extreme longevity and age, the old whale robs them of their final prize. They may take it — and the land they call America — but they cannot keep it; it can never be completely theirs. The word *discovered* is a nicely tricky one. If white men discovered America, who were the "Nor' West Indians," and were they not there first? One has to wonder, sometimes, just who Ishmael really wants to mock.

The next vessel the Pequod meets is a French ship named the Bouton de Rose, or Rosebud. This strange encounter comes "a week or two" after their passage through the lovely Sunda Strait, which links the Indian Ocean to the South China Sea. Ahab's plan is to cruise northward, to . . .

CHAPTER
EIGHTEEN

Ambergris

sweep inshore by the Philippine Islands, and gain the far coast of Japan, in time for the great whaling season there. By these means, the circumnavigating Pequod would sweep almost all the known Sperm Whale cruising grounds of the world, previous to descending upon the Line in the Pacific; where Ahab, though everywhere else foiled in his pursuit, firmly counted upon giving battle to Moby Dick, in the sea he was most known to frequent; and at a season when he might most reasonably be presumed to be haunting it.

The Rosebud, in the first instance, is detected by the whalers' sense of smell—"the many noses on the Pequod's deck proved more vigilant discoverers than the three pairs of eyes aloft," as Ishmael puts it. Alongside her, when she comes into view, the Nantucket men see fastened two "blasted" whales—animals that had died and were quickly decomposing.

It may well be conceived, what an unsavory odor such a mass must exhale. So intolerable indeed is it regarded by some, that no cupidity could persuade them to moor alongside of it. Yet are there those who will still do it; notwithstanding the fact that the oil obtained from such subjects is of a very inferior quality, and by no means of the nature of attar-of-rose.

The reason was that blasted whales—as expert hunters knew—did sometimes contain something worth having: a waxy substance called ambergris, which formed in their diseased digestive systems and was much prized in perfume manufacture. And just in case, the *Pequod*'s gallant Stubb — who has his pipe, of course, to mask the smell — decides to trick the French ship of this (potential) prize, if possible. The captain, he quickly discovers, is on his first voyage and has only fastened on to the dead whales in the hope of getting oil somehow, anyhow. He is quickly convinced that fatal fevers could be caught by breathing such foul air, and Stubb, it being a flat calm day, offers to "help" by towing one of the carcasses clear of the ship. Out of sight behind the *Pequod*, he seizes his sharp boat-spade, and

at once proceeded to reap the fruit of his unrighteous cunning. And all the time numberless fowls were diving, and ducking, and screaming, and yelling, and fighting around them. Stubb was beginning to look disappointed, especially as the horrible nosegay increased, when suddenly from out the very heart of this plague, there stole a faint stream of perfume, which flowed through the tide of bad smells without being absorbed by it.

"I have it, I have it," cried Stubb, with delight, striking something in the subterranean regions, "a purse! a purse!"

Dropping his spade, he thrust both hands in, and drew out handfuls of something that looked like ripe Windsor soap, or rich mottled old cheese; very unctuous and savory withal. And this, good friends, is ambergris, worth a gold guinea an ounce to any druggist. Who would think that fine ladies and gentlemen should regale themselves with an essence found in the inglorious bowels of a sick whale!

Yet so it is.

*I*t was but some few days after encountering the Frenchman, that a most significant event befell the most insignificant of the Pequod's crew; an event most lamentable.

Now, in the whale ship, it is not every one that goes in the boats. Some few hands are reserved called ship-keepers, whose province it is to work the vessel while the boats are pursuing the whale. If there happen to be an unduly slender, clumsy, or timorous wight in the ship, that wight is certain to be made a ship-keeper. It was so in the Pequod with the little negro Pippin by nick-name, Pip by abbreviation. Poor Pip! ye have heard of him before; ye must remember his tambourine on that dramatic midnight, so gloomy-jolly.

C H A P T E R
NINETEEN

*The
Castaway*

Pip, though over tender-hearted, was at bottom very bright, with that pleasant, genial, jolly brightness peculiar to his tribe. Pip loved life, and all life's peaceable securities. But let us to the story.

It came to pass, that in the ambergris affair Stubb's after-oarsman chanced so to sprain his hand, as for a time to become quite maimed; and, temporarily, Pip was put into his place.

Now the boat paddled upon the whale; and as the fish received the darted iron, it gave its customary rap, which happened to be right under poor Pip's seat. The involuntary consternation of the

moment caused him to leap out of the boat; and in such a way, that part of the slack whale line coming against his chest, he breasted it overboard with him, so as to become entangled in it.

Tashtego stood in the bows. He was full of the fire of the hunt. He hated Pip for a poltroon. Snatching the boat-knife from its sheath, he suspended its sharp edge over the line, and turning towards Stubb, exclaimed interrogatively, "Cut?"

"Damn him, cut!" roared Stubb; and so the whale was lost and Pip was saved.

So soon as he recovered himself, the poor little negro was assailed by yells and execrations from the crew. Stubb concluded with a peremptory command, "Stick to the boat, Pip, or by the Lord, I won't pick you up if you jump; mind that. We can't afford to lose whales by the likes of you; a whale would sell for thirty times what you would, Pip, in Alabama. Bear that in mind, and don't jump any more."

But we are all in the hands of the Gods; and Pip jumped again. It was under very similar circumstances; but this time he did not breast out the line; and hence, when the whale started to run, Pip was left behind on the sea. Alas! Stubb was but too true to his word. It was a beautiful, bounteous, blue day; the spangled sea calm and cool, and flatly stretching away, all round, to the horizon, like gold-beater's skin hammered out to the extremest. Bobbing up and down in that sea, Pip's ebon head showed like a head of cloves. In three minutes, a whole mile of shoreless ocean was between Pip and Stubb.

Now, in calm weather, to swim in the open ocean is as easy to the practised swimmer as to ride in a spring-carriage ashore. But the awful lonesomeness is intolerable. The intense concentration of self in the middle of such a heartless immensity, my God! who can tell it? Mark, how when sailors in a dead calm bathe in the open sea—mark how closely they hug their ship and only coast along her sides.

But had Stubb really abandoned the poor little negro to his fate? No; he did not mean to, at least. Because there were two boats in his wake, and he supposed, no doubt, that they would of course come up to Pip very quickly, and

pick him up. But it so happened, that those boats, without seeing Pip, suddenly spying whales close to them on one side, turned, and gave chase.

By the merest chance the ship itself at last rescued him; but from that hour the little negro went about the deck an idiot; such, at least, they said he was. The sea had jeeringly kept his finite body up, but drowned the infinite of his soul. Not drowned entirely, though. Rather carried down alive to wondrous depths, where strange shapes glided to and fro before his passive eyes.

He saw God's foot upon the treadle of the loom, and spoke it; and therefore his shipmates called him mad. So man's insanity is heaven's sense.

For the rest, blame not Stubb too hardly. The thing is common in that fishery; and in the sequel of the narrative, it will then be seen what like abandonment befell myself.

The last "predestinated" foreign vessel the Pequod meets is the Samuel Enderby, of London, and from this ship, at last, comes solid news of Moby-Dick. Once again a particular national characteristic is detected in the English officers — an inability to stop talking! — but mild contempt is mixed, this time, with some respect.

CHAPTER TWENTY

Leg and Arm

Samuel Enderby, for whom the ship was named, originated the famous London whaling house whose ships were the first non-Nantucketers to regularly hunt the sperm whale. They were also the first to fish the Pacific Ocean and the discoverers of the great Japanese whaling ground — although the captain on that momentous voyage was a man named Coffin, a Nantucketer. ⌒ But the clinching argument, for Ahab, that Englishmen are something special, was that this one, Captain Boomer, has not only seen Moby-Dick but has fought with him, and lost his arm.

"Hast seen the White Whale?"

"See you this?" and withdrawing it from the folds that had hidden it, he held up a white arm of sperm whale bone, terminating in a wooden head like a mallet.

⌒ *After this greeting across the water, Ahab goes onboard the English ship. But the two men, although they clash their ivory limbs in comradeship — "let us shake bones together" — cannot share real understanding. Boomer, it transpires, has crossed wakes with Moby Dick again — twice! — but has not tried to kill him, has let him go swimming on his way. When asked why by the scandalized Ahab, he replies, "Ain't one limb enough?"*

"He's welcome to the arm he has, since I can't help it, and didn't know him then; but not to another one. No more White Whales for me; I've lowered for him once, and that has satisfied me. There would be great glory in killing him,

I know that; and there is a ship-load of precious sperm in him, but, hark ye, he's best let alone; don't you think so, Captain?"—glancing at the ivory leg.

"He is. But he will still be hunted, for all that. What is best let alone, that accursed thing is not always what least allures. He's all a magnet! How long since thou saw'st him last? Which way heading?"

"Good God!" cried the English Captain. "What's the matter? He was heading east, I think.—Is your Captain crazy?" whispering Fedallah.

But Fedallah, putting a finger on his lip, slid over the bulwarks to take the boat's steering oar, and Ahab commanded the ship's sailors to stand by to lower.

In a moment he was standing in the boat's stern, and the Manilla men were springing to their oars. In vain the English Captain hailed him. Face set like a flint, Ahab stood upright till alongside of the Pequod.

The precipitating manner in which Captain Ahab had quitted the Samuel Enderby had not been unattended with some small violence to his own person. He had lighted with such energy upon a thwart of his boat that his ivory leg had received a half-splintering shock. He called the carpenter. And when that functionary appeared before him, he bade him without delay set about making a new leg, and directed the mates to see him supplied with all the studs and joists of jaw-ivory (Sperm Whale) which had thus far been accumulated on the voyage, in order that a careful selection of the stoutest, clearest-grained stuff might be secured.

CHAPTER TWENTY-ONE

Ahab's Leg

⟋ This carpenter, Ishmael says, is a pure manipulator. He is like "one of those highly useful Sheffield contrivances, assuming the exterior — though a little swelled — of a common pocket knife, but containing not only blades of various sizes, but also screw-drivers, cork-screws, tweezers, awls, pens, rulers, nail-filers, countersinkers" (what we today would call a Swiss Army knife: Ishmael, it seems, knew better). To this man, making a leg is a routine matter. He can also rebuild smashed boats, pull teeth, repair split masts, make a whalebone cage for an exotic bird that might have flown onboard, paint vermillion stars on Stubb's oarblades, pierce ears for sailors' earrings — anything. By the very next day, Ahab had his leg again — "like a real live leg, filed down to nothing but the core," as the carpenter puts it, with satisfaction. ⟋ Shortly, though, his ingenuity is tested in a most peculiar way — he is asked to make a very special coffin. Unlike most, it is shaped like a South Sea islander's canoe, and unlike almost all, it is destined never to have a dead man's body in it. In fact, it saves a life — although not the life of Queequeg, for whom it is built.

⟿ It happens when the regular twice-weekly check of barrels already filled with precious whale oil and stored down in the hold reveals that some — deep-hidden and unseeable — are leaking. Starbuck, naturally determined to prevent expensive loss, wants Ahab to use the "Burtons" (enormous blocks and tackles) to pull the barrels out, one by one, until the damaged casks are found. Ahab is enraged.

"Up Burtons and break out? Now that we are nearing Japan; heave-to here for a week to tinker with a parcel of old hoops?"

"Either do that, sir, or waste in one day more oil than we may make good in a year. What we come twenty thousand miles to get is worth saving, sir."

"Begone! Let it leak!"

"What will the owners say, sir?"

"Let the owners stand on Nantucket beach and outyell the Typhoons. What cares Ahab? On deck!"

When Starbuck refuses to leave his cabin, Ahab seizes a loaded musket (a rack of guns was always carried in these Eastern waters because of pirates) and levels it at him. For one last time he orders him on deck. Starbuck, without a loss of bravery, decides to give in.

Mastering his emotion, he half calmly rose, and as he quitted the cabin, paused for an instant and said: "Thou hast outraged, not insulted me, sir; but for that I ask thee not to beware of Starbuck; thou wouldst but laugh; but let Ahab beware of Ahab; beware of thyself, old man."

"He waxes brave, but nevertheless obeys; most careful bravery that!" murmured Ahab, as Starbuck disappeared. "What's that he said—Ahab beware of Ahab—there's something there!" Then unconsciously using the musket for a staff, with an iron brow he paced to and fro in the little cabin; but presently the thick plaits of his forehead relaxed, and returning the gun to the rack, he went to the deck.

"Thou art but too good a fellow, Starbuck," he said lowly; then raising his voice to the crew: "Furl the t'gallant-sails, and close-reef the top-sails, fore and aft; back the main-yard; up Burtons, and break out in the main-hold."

The battle of wills, it seems, has been won this time by sanity. But it almost leads to Queequeg's death.

Upon searching, it was found that the casks last struck into the hold were perfectly sound, and that the leak must be further off. So, it being calm weather, they broke out deeper and deeper, disturbing the slumbers of the huge ground-tier butts. Poor Queequeg, as harpooneer, must descend into the gloom of the hold, and bitterly sweating all day in that subterraneous confinement, resolutely manhandle the clumsiest casks and see to their stowage. To be short, among whalemen, the harpooneers are the holders, so called.

CHAPTER TWENTY-TWO

Queequeg in His Coffin

Poor Queequeg! when the ship was about half dis-embowelled, you should have stooped over the hatchway, and peered down upon him there; where, stripped to his woollen drawers, the tattooed savage was crawling about amid that dampness and slime, like a green spotted lizard at the bottom of a well. Where, strange to say, for all the heat of his sweatings, he caught a terrible chill which lapsed into a fever; and at last, after some days' suffering, laid him in his hammock, close to the very sill of the door of death.

Not a man of the crew but gave him up; and, as for Queequeg himself, what he thought of his case was forcibly shown by a curious favor he asked. When this strange circumstance was made known aft, the carpenter was at once commanded to do Queequeg's bidding, whatever it might include. When the last nail was driven, and the lid duly planed and fitted, he lightly shouldered the coffin and went forward with it. Queequeg now entreated to be lifted into his final bed, that he might make trial

of its comforts, if any it had. Then crossing his arms on his breast with Yojo between, he called for the coffin lid (hatch he called it) to be placed over him. But now that he had apparently made every preparation for death; now that his coffin was proved a good fit, Queequeg suddenly rallied; he, in substance, said that he had changed his mind about dying. They asked him, then, whether to live or die was a matter of his own sovereign will and pleasure. He answered, certainly. In a word, it was Queequeg's conceit, that if a man made up his mind to live, mere sickness could not kill him: nothing but a whale, or a gale, or some violent, ungovernable, unintelligent destroyer of that sort.

With a wild whimsiness, he now used his coffin for a sea-chest; and emptying into it his canvas bag of clothes, set them in order there.

When gliding by the Bashee isles we emerged at last upon the great South Sea; that sea in which the hated White Whale must even then be swimming. Launched at length upon these almost final waters, the old man's purpose intensified itself. His firm lips met like the lips of a vice; the Delta of his forehead's veins swelled like overladen brooks; in his very sleep, his ringing cry ran through the vaulted hull, "Stern all! the White Whale spouts thick blood!"

CHAPTER TWENTY-THREE

The Pacific

It is now that Ahab approaches the blacksmith, Perth, to obtain a special harpoon for Moby-Dick. He brings a leather bag of nail stubs from the steel shoes of racing horses —the hardest steel available. Between them, Perth and Ahab forge twelve rods, which they weld into one. Then Ahab gives his razors to the blacksmith to be forged into barbs.

Fashioned at last into an arrowy shape, and welded by Perth to the shank, the steel soon pointed the end of the iron; and as the blacksmith was about giving the barbs their final heat, prior to tempering them, he cried to Ahab to place the water-cask near.

"No, no—no water for that; I want it of the true death-temper. Ahoy, there! Tashtego, Queequeg, Daggoo! What say ye, pagans! Will ye give me as much blood as will cover this barb?" holding it high up. A cluster of dark nods replied, Yes. Three punctures were made in the heathen flesh, and the White Whale's barbs were then tempered.

"Ego non baptizo te in nomine patris, sed in nomine diaboli!"
[I do not baptize thee in the name of the Father, but in the name of the Devil]
howled Ahab, as iron scorchingly devoured the baptismal blood.

This done, Ahab moodily stalked away
with the weapon; the sound of his ivory leg,
and the sound of the hickory pole, both
hollowly ringing along every plank.
But ere he entered his cabin, a light,
unnatural, half-bantering, yet
most piteous sound was heard.
Oh, Pip! thy wretched laugh,
thy idle but unresting eye; all
thy strange mummeries not
unmeaningly blended with
the black tragedy of the
melancholy ship, and
mocked it!

*J*olly enough were the sights and the sounds that came bearing down before the wind, some few weeks after Ahab's harpoon had been welded.

It was a Nantucket ship, the Bachelor, which had just wedged in her last cask of oil, and bolted down her bursting hatches; and now, in glad holiday apparel, was joyously sailing round among the widely-separated ships on the ground, previous to pointing her prow for home.

CHAPTER
TWENTY-FOUR

*The Pequod
Meets the
Bachelor*

The three men at her mast-head wore long streamers of narrow red bunting at their hats; from the stern, a whale-boat was suspended; and hanging captive from the bowsprit was seen the long lower jaw of the last whale they had slain. Signals, ensigns, and jacks of all colors were flying from her rigging, on every side. Sideways lashed in each of her three basketed tops were two barrels of sperm; above which, in her top-mast cross-trees, you saw slender breakers of the same precious fluid; and nailed to her main truck was a brazen lamp.

As this glad ship of good luck bore down upon the moody Pequod, the barbarian sound of enormous drums came from her forecastle; and drawing still nearer, a crowd of her men were seen standing round her huge try-pots, which, covered with the parchment-like *poke* or stomach skin of the black fish, gave forth a loud roar to every stroke of the clenched hands of the crew. On the quarter-deck, the mates and harpooneers were dancing with the olive-hued girls who had eloped with them from the Polynesian Isles; while suspended in an ornamented boat, firmly secured aloft between the foremast and mainmast, three Long Island negroes, with glittering fiddle-bows of whale ivory, were presiding over the hilarious jig.

Lord and master over all this scene, the captain stood erect on the ship's elevated quarter-deck, so that the whole rejoicing drama was full before him, and seemed merely contrived for his own individual diversion.

And Ahab, he too was standing on his quarter-deck, shaggy and black, with a stubborn gloom.

"Come aboard, come aboard!" cried the gay Bachelor's commander, lifting a glass and a bottle in the air.

"Hast seen the White Whale?" gritted Ahab in reply.

"No; only heard of him; but don't believe in him at all," said the other good-humoredly. "Come aboard!"

"Thou art too damned jolly. Sail on."

Next day after encountering the Bachelor, whales were seen and four were slain; one far to windward. Three were brought alongside ere nightfall; but the windward one could not be reached till morning; and the boat that had killed it lay by its side all night; and that boat was Ahab's.

The waif-pole was thrust upright into the dead whale's spout-hole; and the lantern hanging from its top, cast a troubled flickering glare upon the black, glossy back, and far out upon the midnight waves, which gently chafed the whale's broad flank, like soft surf upon a beach.

Started from his slumbers, Ahab, face to face, saw the Parsee; and hooped round by the gloom of the night they seemed the last men in a flooded world. "I have dreamed it again," said he.

"Of the hearses? Have I not said, old man, that neither hearse nor coffin can be thine?"

"And who are hearsed that die on the sea?"

"But I said, old man, that ere thou couldst die on this voyage, two hearses must verily be seen by thee on the sea; the first not made by mortal hands; and the visible wood of the last one must be grown in America."

"And what was that saying about thyself?"

"Though it come to the last, I shall still go before thee thy pilot."

"And when thou art so gone before then ere I can follow, thou must still appear to me, to pilot me still? Well, then, I have here two pledges that I shall yet slay Moby Dick and survive it."

"Take another pledge, old man," said the Parsee, as his eyes lighted up like fire-flies in the gloom—"Hemp only can kill thee."

"The gallows, ye mean.—I am immortal then, on land and on sea," cried Ahab, with a laugh of derision;—"Immortal on land and on sea!"

Both were silent again, as one man. The grey dawn came on, and the slumbering crew arose from the boat's bottom, and ere noon the dead whale was brought to the ship.

For all Ahab's hopes — convictions even — that he is to all intents immortal, the sense of doom and deep foreboding grows on the Pequod as the season for the Line approaches. They are moving ever deeper into the Pacific Ocean, and the men console themselves by dreaming that the doubloon nailed to the mast is waiting to be won.

Ahab's torments, though, become ever more apparent. One day he smashes the quadrant, used to fix position by sun and star sights, with the startling cry of "Science! Curse thee, thou vain toy!" From henceforward, he declares, he will rely solely on the log line, which measures distance covered, and the compass, for the ship's direction. Very shortly, horribly, the compass lets him down. Before that, though, on the very day he smashes the quadrant, the ship is beset by a terrible hurricane, which brings them Saint Elmo's fire (which Starbuck calls the corposants), a phenomenon that occurs at sea in violent electrical disturbances and that sailors perceived in those times as the very worst of portents. In the area where the Pequod is sailing, the type of storm that struck her is known as a typhoon. She is taken from dead ahead, stripped of her canvas by the wind, and left to fight bare-poled.

CHAPTER
TWENTY-FIVE

The Candles

When darkness came on, sky and sea roared and split with the thunder, and blazed with the lightning, that showed the disabled masts fluttering here and there with the rags which the first fury of the tempest had left for its after sport.

Holding by a shroud, Starbuck was standing on the quarter-deck; at every flash of the lightning glancing aloft, to see what additional disaster might have befallen the intricate hamper there; while Stubb and Flask were directing the men in the higher hoisting and firmer lashing of the boats. But all their pains seemed naught. Though lifted to the very top of the cranes, the windward quarter boat (Ahab's) did not escape. A great rolling sea, dashing high up against the reeling ship's high teetering side, stove in the boat's bottom at the stern, and left it again, all dripping through like a sieve.

"Look aloft!" cried Starbuck. "The corpusants! the corpusants!"

All the yard-arms were tipped with a pallid fire; and touched at each tri-pointed lightning-rod-end with three tapering white flames, each of the three tall masts was silently burning in that sulphurous air, like three gigantic wax tapers before an altar.

While this pallidness was burning aloft, few words were heard from the enchanted crew; who in one thick cluster stood on the forecastle, all their eyes gleaming in that pale phosphorescence, like a far away constellation of stars. Relieved against the ghostly light, the gigantic jet negro, Daggoo, loomed up to thrice his real stature, and seemed the black cloud from which the thunder had come. The parted mouth of Tashtego revealed his shark-white teeth, which strangely gleamed as if they too had been tipped by corpusants; while lit up by the preternatural light, Queequeg's tattooing burned like Satanic blue flames on his body.

At the base of the mainmast, the Parsee was kneeling in Ahab's front, with his head bowed away from him.

"Aye, aye, men!" cried Ahab. "Look up at it; mark it well; the white flame but lights the way to the White Whale! Hand me those main-mast links there; I would fain feel this pulse, and let mine beat against it; blood against fire! So."

Then turning—the last link held fast in his left hand, he put his foot upon the Parsee; and with fixed upward eye, and high-flung right arm, he stood erect before the lofty tri-pointed trinity of flames.

"The boat! the boat!" cried Starbuck, "look at thy boat, old man!"

Ahab's harpoon, the one forged at Perth's fire, remained firmly lashed in its conspicuous crotch, so that it projected beyond his whale-boat's bow; but the sea that had stove its bottom had caused the loose leather sheath to drop off; and from the keen steel barb there now came a levelled flame of pale, forked fire. As the silent harpoon burned there like a serpent's tongue, Starbuck grasped Ahab by the arm—"God, God is against thee, old man; forbear! 't is an ill voyage! ill begun, ill continued; let me square the yards, while we may, old man, and make a fair wind of it homewards, to go on a better voyage than this."

Overhearing Starbuck, the panic-stricken crew instantly ran to the braces— though not a sail was left aloft. For the moment all the aghast mate's thoughts seemed theirs; they raised a half mutinous cry. But snatching the burning harpoon, Ahab waved it like a torch among them; swearing to transfix with it the first sailor that but cast loose a rope's end. Petrified by his aspect, and still more shrinking from the fiery dart that he held, the men fell back in dismay, and Ahab again spoke:—

"All your oaths to hunt the White Whale are as binding as mine; and heart, soul, and body, lungs and life, old Ahab is bound. And that ye may know to what tune this heart beats: look ye here; thus I blow out the last fear!" And with one blast of his breath he extinguished the flame.

At those last words of Ahab's many of the mariners did run from him in a terror of dismay. ⬡

Despite Starbuck's pleas that when the "corpusants" burn out, they should "send down" yards and other heavyweight gear from high up the masts because the ship is in such deadly danger from the wind, Ahab mocks and insults him. "None but cowards," he shouts, "send down in tempest time!" It is clear to Starbuck, as to all other thinking men onboard, that Ahab is prepared to defy God himself, let alone the weather, to confront his destiny. And when the weather eases, some hours after midnight, it is with heavy heart indeed that the pious mate bends on new sails and reefs them down and gets the *Pequod* sailing fair again. Then, to complete his feeling of despair, when the helmsman gets the ship back onto her intended course, it is discovered by the compass that the wind changed completely in the wildness of the storm. It was foul, but now is fair. The yards are trimmed to the new breeze, the crew sings with joy, and Starbuck, as he is required to, goes below to report how things have altered. They have a proper wind, once more, to take them to destruction. The captain is sleeping in his cabin, his head protected from a bullet merely by a thin, light, wooden-paneled door. "Honest, upright" Starbuck, taken by "an evil thought," picks up a loaded musket from the nearby rack — the very gun, he recognizes, that Ahab leveled at him not long before — and fights a bitter battle with his Christian conscience. He can kill the old man or let him "drag a whole ship's company down to doom with him; make him the murderer of thirty men and more." He knows he cannot withstand Ahab and that Ahab will be awake very soon. He agonizes.

CHAPTER
TWENTY-SIX

The Musket

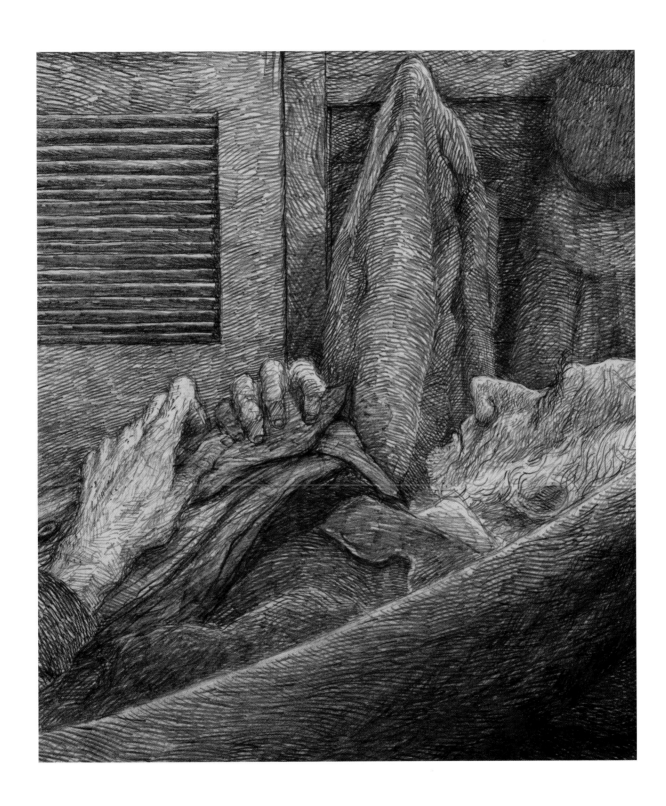

"But is there no other way? no lawful way?—Make him a prisoner to be taken home? What! hope to wrest this old man's living power from his own living hands? Only a fool would try it. Say he were pinioned even; knotted all over with ropes and hawsers; chained down to ring-bolts on this cabin floor; he would be more hideous than a caged tiger, then. I could not endure the sight. What, then, remains? The land is hundreds of leagues away, and locked Japan the nearest. I stand alone here upon an open sea, with two oceans and a whole continent between me and law.—Aye, aye, 'tis so.—Is heaven a murderer when its lightning strikes a would-be murderer in his bed, tindering sheets and skin together?—And would I be a murderer, then, if"—and slowly, stealthily, and half sideways looking, he placed the loaded musket's end against the door.

"On this level, Ahab's hammock swings within; his head this way. A touch, and Starbuck may survive to hug his wife and child again.—Oh, Mary! Mary!—boy! boy! boy!—But if I wake thee not to death, old man, who can tell to what unsounded deeps Starbuck's body this day week may sink, with all the crew! Great God, where art thou? Shall I? shall I?—"

The yet levelled musket shook like a drunkard's arm against the panel; Starbuck seemed wrestling with an angel; but turning from the door, he placed the death-tube in its rack, and left the place.

"He's too sound asleep. Mr. Stubb; go thou down, and wake him, and tell him. I must see to the deck here. Thou know'st what to say."

That very morning, as the blazing sun is rising, there is another sign, or portent. Again, Ahab turns it to his advantage with his superstitious crew. He — and no other man onboard — realizes that it is not the wind that changed in the typhoon but the compass. The discharges of the electrical storm reversed the polarity of the needle, so that north reads south, east reads west, and so on. Far from heading farther toward where Moby-Dick must be, the Pequod is, effectively, with a good fair wind, being blown away from him. Furious, the captain orders that the ship's course be altered back again, and although many of the crew are fearful now at meeting their awful destiny, "their fear of Ahab was greater than their fear of Fate." Ahab, also, in his many years at sea, has seen such things before and knows that he can easily magnetize and fit a new needle to the compass — and deliberately stage a piece of "magic" to retain his power over them. He calls his mate to bring some simple items with which to work his "spell."

CHAPTER
TWENTY-SEVEN

The
Life-Buoy

"Mr. Starbuck—a lance without the pole; a top-maul, and the smallest of the sail-maker's needles. Quick!"

With a blow from the top-maul Ahab knocked off the steel head of the lance, then placed the blunted needle endwise on the top of it, and less strongly hammered that, the mate holding the rod. Then going through some small strange motions with it—whether indispensable to the magnetizing of the steel, or merely intended to augment the awe of the crew, is uncertain— he called for linen thread; and moving to the binnacle, slipped out the two reversed needles there, and horizontally suspended the sail-needle by its middle, over one of the compass-cards. At first, the steel went round and round, quivering and vibrating at either end; but at last it settled to its place, when Ahab, who had been intently watching for this result, stepped frankly back from the binnacle, and pointing his stretched arm towards it, exclaimed,—"Look ye, for yourselves, if Ahab be not lord of the level load-stone! The sun is East, and that compass swears it!"

One after another they peered in, for nothing but their own eyes could persuade such ignorance as theirs, and one after another they slunk away.

In his fiery eyes of scorn and triumph, you then saw Ahab in all his fatal pride.

Steering now south-eastward by Ahab's levelled steel, and her progress solely determined by Ahab's level log and line; the Pequod held on her path towards the Equator. But the bodings of the crew were destined to receive a most plausible confirmation in the fate of one of their number. This man went to his mast-head at the fore; but had not been long at his perch, when a cry was heard—a cry and a rushing—and looking up, they saw a falling phantom in the air; and looking down, a little tossed heap of white bubbles in the blue of the sea.

The life-buoy—a long slender cask—was dropped from the stern, where it always hung obedient to a cunning spring; but no hand rose to seize it, and the sun having long beat upon this cask it had shrunken, so that it slowly filled, and the parched wood also filled at its every pore; and the studded iron-bound cask followed the sailor to the bottom, as if to yield him his pillow, though in sooth but a hard one.

And thus the first man of the Pequod that mounted the mast to look out for the White Whale, on the White Whale's own peculiar ground; that man was swallowed up in the deep.

The lost life-buoy was now to be replaced; but as no cask of sufficient lightness could be found, they were going to leave the ship's stern unprovided, when by certain strange signs and inuendoes Queequeg hinted a hint concerning his coffin.

"A life-buoy of a coffin!" cried Starbuck, starting.

"Rather queer, that, I should say," said Stubb.

"It will make a good enough one," said Flask, "the carpenter here can arrange it easily."

"Bring it up; there's nothing else for it," said Starbuck, after a melancholy pause. "Rig it, carpenter; do not look at me so—the coffin, I mean. Dost thou hear me? Rig it."

"And shall I nail down the lid, sir?" moving his hand as with a hammer.

"Aye."

"And shall I caulk the seams, sir?" moving his hand as with a caulking-iron.

"Aye."

"And shall I then pay over the same with pitch, sir?" moving his hand as with a pitch-pot.

"Away! what possesses thee to this? Make a life-buoy of the coffin, and no more."

"'Hem! I'll do the job, now, tenderly. I'll have me thirty separate, Turk's-headed life-lines, each three feet long hanging all round to the coffin. Then, if the hull go down, there'll be thirty lively fellows all fighting for one coffin, a sight not seen very often beneath the sun! Let's to it."

Next day, a large ship, the Rachel, was descried, all her spars thickly clustering with men. But ere her commander, who, with trumpet to mouth, stood up in his boat; ere he could hopefully hail, Ahab's voice was heard.

"Hast seen the White Whale?"

CHAPTER
TWENTY-EIGHT

*The Pequod
Meets the
Rachel*

"Aye, yesterday. Have ye seen a whale-boat adrift?"

Throttling his joy, Ahab negatively answered this unexpected question; and would then have fain boarded the stranger, when the stranger captain himself was seen descending her side. A few keen pulls, and his boat-hook soon clinched the Pequod's main-chains, and he sprang to the deck. Immediately he was recognised by Ahab for a Nantucketer he knew. But no formal salutation was exchanged.

"Where was he?—not killed!—not killed!" cried Ahab, closely advancing. "How was it?"

It seemed that somewhat late the day previous, while three of the stranger's boats were engaged with a shoal of whales, which had led them some four or five miles from the ship; and while they were yet in swift chase to windward, the white hump and head of Moby Dick had suddenly loomed up out of the blue water, not very far to leeward; whereupon, the fourth rigged boat—a reserved one—had been instantly lowered in chase. After a keen sail, this fourth boat seemed to have succeeded in fastening —at least, as well as the man at the mast-head could tell anything about it. In the distance he saw the diminished dotted boat; and then a swift gleam of bubbling white water; and after that nothing more; whence it was concluded that the stricken whale must have indefinitely run away with his pursuers, as often happens. There was some apprehension, but no positive alarm, as yet. The recall signals were placed in the rigging; darkness came on; and forced to pick up her three far to windward boats, the ship had not only been necessitated to leave that boat to its fate till near midnight, but, for the time, to increase her distance from it. But the rest of her crew being at last safe aboard, she crowded all sail after the missing boat. But though when she had thus sailed a sufficient distance to gain the presumed place of the absent ones when last seen; though she then paused to lower her spare boats to pull all around her; and not finding anything, had again dashed on; again paused, and lowered her boats; and though she had thus continued doing till day light; yet not the least glimpse of the missing keel had been seen.

The story told, the stranger Captain immediately went on to reveal his object in boarding the Pequod. He desired that ship to unite with his own in the search; by sailing over the sea some four or five miles apart, on parallel lines, and so sweeping a double horizon, as it were.

"My boy, my own boy is among them. For God's sake—I beg, I conjure— for eight-and-forty hours let me charter your ship—I will gladly pay for it, and roundly pay for it—if there be no other way—for eight-and-forty hours only—only that—you must, oh, you must, and you *shall* do this thing."

"His son!" cried Stubb, "oh, it's his son he's lost! What says Ahab? We must save that boy."

⌐ The child, they learn, is twelve years old. But Ahab "still stood like an anvil, receiving every shock, but without the least quivering of his own."

"I will not go," said the stranger, "till you say *aye* to me. Yes, yes, you relent; I see it—run, run, men, now, and stand by to square in the yards."

"Avast," cried Ahab—"touch not a rope-yarn"; then in a voice that prolongingly moulded every word—"Captain Gardiner, I will not do it.

Even now I lose time. Goodbye, goodbye. God bless ye, man, and may I forgive myself, but I must go."

Soon the two ships diverged their wakes; and long as the strange vessel was in view, she was seen to yaw hither and thither at every dark spot, however small, on the sea. This way and that her yards were swung round; starboard and larboard, she continued to tack; now she beat against a head sea; and again it pushed her before it; while all the while, her masts and yards were thickly clustered with men, as three tall cherry trees, when the boys are cherrying among the boughs.

But by her still halting course and winding, woful way, you plainly saw that this ship that so wept with spray, still remained without comfort. She was Rachel, weeping for her children, because they were not.

The intense Pequod sailed on; the rolling waves and days went by; the life-buoy-coffin still lightly swung; and another ship, most miserably misnamed the Delight, was descried. As she drew nigh, all eyes were fixed upon her broad beams, called shears, which, in some whaling-ships, cross the quarter-deck at the height of eight or nine feet; serving to carry the spare, unrigged, or disabled boats.

CHAPTER
TWENTY-NINE

*The Pequod
Meets the
Delight*

Upon the stranger's shears were beheld the shattered, white ribs, and some few splintered planks, of what had once been a whale-boat; but you now saw through this wreck, as plainly as you see through the peeled, half-unhinged, and bleaching skeleton of a horse.

"Hast seen the White Whale?"

"Look!" replied the hollow-cheeked captain from his taffrail; and with his trumpet he pointed to the wreck.

"Hast killed him?"

"The harpoon is not yet forged that will ever do that," answered the other, sadly glancing upon a rounded hammock on the deck, whose gathered sides some noiseless sailors were busy in sewing together.

"Not forged!" and snatching Perth's levelled iron from the crotch, Ahab held it out, exclaiming—"Look ye, Nantucketer; here in this hand I hold his death! Tempered in blood, and tempered by lightning are these barbs; and I swear to temper them triply in that hot place behind the fin, where the White Whale most feels his accursed life!"

"Then God keep thee, old man—see'st thou that"—pointing to the hammock—"I bury but one of five stout men, who were alive only yesterday; but were dead ere night. Only *that* one I bury; the rest were buried before they died; you sail upon their tomb." Then turning to his crew—"Are ye ready there? place the plank then on the rail, and lift the body; so, then— Oh! God"—advancing towards the hammock with uplifted hands—"may the resurrection and the life—"

"Brace forward! Up helm!" cried Ahab like lightning to his men.

But the suddenly started Pequod was not quick enough to escape the sound of the splash that the corpse soon made as it struck the sea; not so quick, indeed, but that some of the flying bubbles might have sprinkled her hull with their ghostly baptism.

As Ahab now glided from the dejected Delight, the strange life-buoy hanging at the Pequod's stern came into conspicuous relief.

"Ha! yonder! look yonder, men!" cried a foreboding voice in her wake. "In vain, oh, ye strangers, ye fly our sad burial; ye but turn us your taffrail to show us your coffin!"

It was a clear steel-blue day. The firmaments of air and sea were hardly separable in that all-pervading azure. Slowly crossing the deck from the scuttle, Ahab leaned over the side, and watched how his shadow in the water sank and sank to his gaze, the more and the more that he strove to pierce the profundity.

CHAPTER THIRTY

The Symphony

But the lovely aromas in that enchanted air did at last seem to dispel, for a moment, the cankerous thing in his soul. From beneath his slouched hat Ahab dropped a tear into the sea; nor did all the Pacific contain such wealth as that one wee drop.

Starbuck saw the old man; saw him, how he heavily leaned over the side; and he seemed to hear in his own true heart the measureless sobbing that stole out of the centre of the serenity around. Careful not to touch him, or be noticed by him, he yet drew near to him, and stood there.

Ahab turned.

"Starbuck!"

"Sir."

"Oh, Starbuck! it is a mild, mild wind, and a mild looking sky. On such a day—very much such a sweetness as this— I struck my first whale—a boy-harpooneer of eighteen! Forty—forty—forty years ago! Forty years of continual whaling! forty years of privation, and peril, and stormtime! Aye and yes, Starbuck, out of those forty years I have not spent three ashore. When I think of this life I have led; the desolation of solitude it has been; oh, weariness! heaviness! Away, whole oceans away, from that young girl-wife I wedded past fifty, and sailed for Cape Horn the next day, leaving but one dent in my marriage pillow—wife? wife?—rather a widow with her husband alive! Aye, I widowed that poor girl when I married her, Starbuck; aye, aye! what a forty years' fool—fool—old fool, has old Ahab been! Oh, Starbuck! is it not hard, that with this weary load I bear, one poor leg should have been snatched from under me? Here, brush this old hair aside; it blinds me, that I seem to weep. Locks so grey did never grow but from out some ashes! But do I look very old, so very, very old, Starbuck? I feel deadly faint, bowed, and humped, as though I were Adam, staggering beneath the piled centuries since Paradise. Close! stand close to me, Starbuck; let me look into a human eye; it is better than to gaze into sea or sky; better than to gaze upon God. This is the magic glass, man; I see my wife and my child in thine eye. No, no; stay on board, on board!—lower not when I do; when branded Ahab gives chase to Moby Dick. That hazard shall not be thine. No, no! not with the far away home I see in that eye!"

"Oh, my Captain! my Captain! noble soul! grand old heart, after all! why should any one give chase to that hated fish! Away with me! let us fly these deadly waters! let us home! Wife and child, too, are Starbuck's—wife and child even as thine, sir. Away! let us away!—this instant let me alter the course! How cheerily, how hilariously, O my Captain, would we bowl on our way to see old Nantucket again! I think, sir, they have some such mild blue days, even as this, in Nantucket."

"They have, they have. I have seen them—some summer days in the morning. About this time—yes, it is his noon nap now—the boy vivaciously wakes; sits up in bed; and his mother tells him of me, of cannibal old me; how I am abroad upon the deep, but will yet come back to dance him again."

"'Tis my Mary, my Mary herself! She promised that my boy, every morning, should be carried to the hill to catch the first glimpse of his father's sail! Yes, yes! no more! it is done! we head for Nantucket! Come, my Captain, study out the course, and let us away! See, see! the boy's face from the window! the boy's hand on the hill!"

But Ahab's glance was averted; like a blighted fruit tree he
shook, and cast his last, cindered apple to the soil.
"What is it, what nameless, inscrutable, unearthly thing is it; what
cozening hidden lord and master, and cruel, remorseless emperor
commands me; that against all natural lovings and longings, I so keep
pushing, and crowding, and jamming myself on all the time?
By heaven, man, we are turned round and round in this world,
like yonder windlass, and Fate is the handspike. But it is a mild,
mild wind, and a mild looking sky; and the air smells now,
as if it blew from a far-away meadow; they have been
making hay somewhere under the slopes of
the Andes, Starbuck, and the mowers are
sleeping among the new-mown hay.
Sleeping? Aye, toil we how we may,
we all sleep at last on the field. Sleep?
Aye, and rust amid greenness; as last
year's scythes flung down, and left
in the half-cut swaths — Starbuck!"
But blanched to a corpse's hue with
despair, the Mate had stolen away.
Ahab crossed the deck to gaze over
on the other side; but started at
two reflected, fixed eyes in
the water there. Fedallah was
motionlessly leaning over
the same rail.

That night, in the mid-watch, when the old man stepped forth from the scuttle and went to his pivot-hole, he suddenly thrust out his face fiercely, snuffing up the sea air as a sagacious ship's dog will, in drawing nigh to some barbarous isle. He declared that a whale must be near. Soon that peculiar odor, sometimes to a great distance given forth by the living sperm whale, was palpable to all the watch; nor was any mariner surprised when Ahab rapidly ordered the ship's course to be slightly altered, and the sail to be shortened.

CHAPTER
THIRTY-ONE

*The Chase—
First Day*

The acute policy dictating these movements was sufficiently vindicated at daybreak, by the sight of a long sleek on the sea directly and lengthwise ahead, smooth as oil, and resembling the polished metallic-like marks of some swift tide-rip.

"Man the mast-heads! Call all hands!"

All sail being set, he now cast loose the life-line, reserved for swaying him to the main royal-mast head; and in a few moments they were hoisting him thither, when, peering ahead, he raised a gull-like cry in the air, "There she blows!—there she blows! A hump like a snow-hill! It is Moby Dick!"

Fired by the cry which seemed simultaneously taken up by the three look-outs, the men on deck rushed to the rigging to behold the famous whale they had so long been pursuing. Ahab had now gained his final perch, some feet above the other look-outs, Tashtego standing just beneath him on the cap of the top-gallant-mast, so that the Indian's head was almost on a level with Ahab's heel. From this height the whale was now seen some mile or so ahead, at every roll of the sea revealing his high sparkling hump, and regularly jetting his silent spout into the air. To the credulous mariners it seemed the same silent spout they had so long ago beheld in the moonlit Atlantic and Indian Oceans.

"And did none of ye see it before?" cried Ahab, hailing the perched men all around him.

"I saw him almost that same instant, sir, that Captain Ahab did, and I cried out," said Tashtego.

"Not the same instant; not the same—no, the doubloon is mine, Fate reserved the doubloon for me. *I* only; none of ye could have raised the White Whale first. There she blows! there she blows!—there she blows! There again—there again!" he cried, in long-drawn, lingering, methodic tones, attuned to the gradual prolongings of the whale's visible jets. "He's going to sound! Stand by three boats. Mr. Starbuck, remember, stay on board, and keep the ship. Lower me, Mr. Starbuck; lower, lower,—quick, quicker!" and he slid through the air to the deck.

Soon all the boats but Starbuck's were dropped; and Ahab heading the onset. A pale, death-glimmer lit up Fedallah's sunken eyes; a hideous motion gnawed his mouth.

Like noiseless nautilus shells, their light prows sped through the sea; but only slowly they neared the foe. As they neared him, the ocean grew still more smooth; seemed drawing a carpet over its waves; seemed a noon-meadow, so serenely it spread. At length the breathless hunter came so nigh his seemingly unsuspecting prey, that his entire dazzling hump was distinctly visible, sliding along the sea as if an isolated thing, and continually set in a revolving ring of finest, fleecy, greenish foam. He saw the vast, involved wrinkles of the slightly projecting head beyond. Before it, far out on the soft Turkish-rugged waters, went the glistening white shadow from his broad, milky forehead, a musical rippling playfully accompanying the shade; and behind, the blue waters interchangeably flowed over into the moving valley of his steady wake; and on either hand bright bubbles arose and danced by his side.

And thus, through the serene tranquillities of the tropical sea, Moby Dick moved on, still withholding from sight the full terrors of his submerged trunk, entirely hiding the wrenched hideousness of his jaw. But soon the fore part of him slowly rose from the water; for an instant his whole marbleized body formed a high arch, and warningly waving his bannered flukes in the air, the grand god revealed himself, sounded, and went out of sight. White sea-fowls longingly lingered over the agitated pool that he left.

With oars apeak, and paddles down, the sheets of their sails adrift, the three boats now stilly floated, awaiting Moby Dick's reappearance.

"An hour," said Ahab, standing rooted in his boat's stern; and he gazed beyond the whale's place, towards the dim blue spaces and wide wooing vacancies to leeward. The breeze now freshened; the sea began to swell.

"The birds!—the birds!" cried Tashtego.

In long Indian file, as when herons take wing, the white birds were now all flying towards Ahab's boat; and when within a few yards began fluttering over the water there, wheeling round and round, with joyous, expectant cries. Their vision was keener than man's; Ahab could discover no sign in the sea.

But suddenly as he peered down and down into its depths, he profoundly saw a white living spot with wonderful celerity uprising, and magnifying as it rose, till it turned, and then there were plainly revealed two long crooked rows of white, glistening teeth, floating up from the undiscoverable bottom. It was Moby Dick's open mouth and scrolled jaw; his vast, shadowed bulk still half blending with the blue of the sea. The glittering mouth yawned beneath the boat like an open-doored marble tomb; and giving one sidelong sweep with his steering oar, Ahab whirled the craft aside from this tremendous apparition. Then, calling upon Fedallah to change places with him, went forward to the bows, and seizing Perth's harpoon, commanded his crew to grasp their oars and stand by to stern.

Now, by reason of this timely spinning round the boat upon its axis, its bow, by anticipation, was made to face the whale's head while yet under water. But as if perceiving this stratagem, Moby Dick, with that malicious intelligence ascribed to him, sidelingly transplanted himself, as it were, in an instant, shooting his pleated head lengthwise beneath the boat.

Through and through; through every plank and each rib, it thrilled for an instant, the whale obliquely lying on his back, in the manner of a biting shark, slowly and feelingly taking its bows full within his mouth, so that the long, narrow, scrolled lower jaw curled high up into the open air, and one of the teeth caught in a row-lock. The bluish pearl-white of the inside of the jaw was within six inches of Ahab's head, and reached higher than that. In this attitude the White Whale now shook the slight cedar as a mildly cruel cat her mouse. With unastonished eyes Fedallah gazed, and crossed his arms; but the tiger-yellow crew were tumbling over each other's heads to gain the uttermost stern.

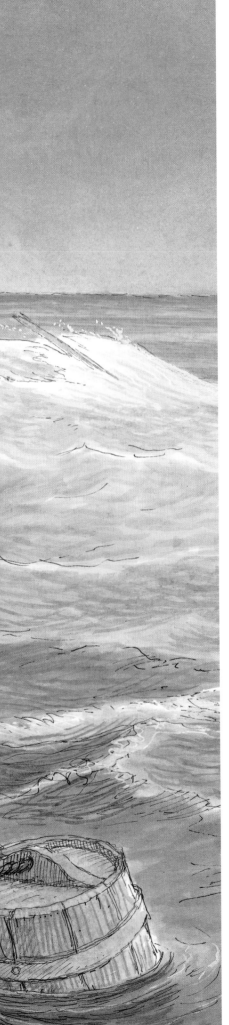

And now, while both elastic gunwales were springing in and out, as the whale dallied with the doomed craft in this devilish way; then it was that monomaniac Ahab seized the long bone with his naked hands, and wildly strove to wrench it from its gripe. The jaw slipped from him; the frail gunwales bent in, collapsed, and snapped, as both jaws, like an enormous shears, bit the craft completely in twain, and locked themselves fast again in the sea, midway between the two floating wrecks.

Ripplingly withdrawing from his prey, Moby Dick now lay at a little distance, vertically thrusting his oblong white head up and down in the billows; and at the same time slowly revolving his whole spindled body.

But soon resuming his horizontal attitude, Moby Dick swam swiftly round and round the wrecked crew; churning the water in his vengeful wake, as if lashing himself up to still another and more deadly assault. Helpless Ahab's head was seen, like a tossed bubble which the least chance shock might burst. From the boat's fragmentary stern, Fedallah incuriously and mildly eyed him; the clinging crew, at the other drifting end, could not succor him. And though the other boats, unharmed, still hovered hard by; they dared not pull into the eddy to strike, lest that should be the signal for the instant destruction of the castaways, Ahab and all. With straining eyes, then, they remained on the outer edge of the direful zone, whose centre had now become the old man's head.

Meantime, from the beginning all this had been descried from the ship's mastheads; and squaring her yards, she had borne down upon the scene; and was now so nigh, that Ahab in the water hailed her;—"Sail on the whale!—Drive him off!"

The Pequod's prow was pointed; and breaking up the charmed circle, she effectually parted the white whale from his victim. As he sullenly swam off, the boats flew to the rescue.

Dragged into Stubb's boat with blood-shot, blinded eyes, the white brine caking in his wrinkles; the long tension of Ahab's bodily strength did crack, and helplessly he yielded to his body's doom: for a time. Nameless wails came from him, as desolate sounds from out ravines.

"The harpoon," said Ahab, half way rising, and draggingly leaning on one bended arm—"is it safe?"

"Aye, sir, for it was not darted; this is it," said Stubb, showing it.

"Lay it before me;—any missing men?"

"One, two, three, four, five;—there were five oars, sir, and here are five men."

"That's good.—Help me, man; I wish to stand. So, so, I see him! there! going to leeward still; what a leaping spout!—Hands off from me! The eternal sap runs up in Ahab's bones again! Set the sail; out oars; the helm!"

It is often the case that when a boat is stove, its crew, being picked up by another boat, help to work that second boat; and the chase is thus continued with what is called double-banked oars. It was thus now. But the added power of the boat did not equal the added power of the whale, for he seemed to have treble-banked his every fin. The ship itself, then, offered the most promising means of overtaking the chase. Accordingly, the boats now made for her, and were soon swayed up to their cranes—the two parts of the wrecked boat having been previously secured by her—and then hoisting everything to her side, and stacking her canvas high up, and sideways outstretching it with stun-sails, like the double-jointed wings of an albatross; the Pequod bore down in the leeward wake of Moby Dick. At the well known, methodic intervals, the whale's glittering spout was regularly announced from the manned mast-heads; and when he would be reported as just gone down, Ahab would take the time, and then pacing the deck, binnacle-watch in hand, so soon as the last second of the allotted hour expired, his voice was heard.—"Whose is the doubloon now? D'ye see him?" and if the reply was, No, sir! straightway he commanded them to lift him to his perch. In this way the day wore on; Ahab, now aloft and motionless; anon, unrestingly pacing the planks.

Soon, it was almost dark.

"Can't see the spout now, sir;—too dark"—cried a voice from the air.

"How heading when last seen?"

"As before, sir,—straight to leeward."

"Good! he will travel slower now 'tis night. Down royals and top-gallant stun-sails, Mr. Starbuck. We must not run over him before morning. Aloft! come down!—Mr. Stubb, send a fresh hand to the fore-mast head, and see it manned till morning."—Then advancing towards the doubloon in the main-mast—"Men, this gold is mine, for I earned it; but I shall let it abide here till the White Whale is dead; and then, whosoever of ye first raises him, upon the day he shall be killed, this gold is that man's; and if on that day I shall again raise him, then, ten times its sum shall be divided among all of ye! Away now!—the deck is thine, sir."

And so saying, he placed himself half way within the scuttle, and slouching his hat, stood there till dawn.

At day-break, the three mast-heads were punctually manned afresh.

"D'ye see him?" cried Ahab, after allowing a little space for the light to spread.

"See nothing, sir."

"Turn up all hands and make sail! he travels faster than I thought for;—the top-gallant sails!—aye, they should have been kept on her all night. But no matter—'tis but resting for the rush."

The ship tore on; leaving such a furrow in the sea as when a cannon-ball, missent, becomes a plough-share and turns up the level field.

"By salt and hemp!" cried Stubb, "but this swift motion of the deck creeps up one's legs and tingles at the heart. This ship and I are two brave fellows!—Ha! ha! Some one take me up, and launch me, spine-wise, on the sea,—for by live-oaks! my spine's a keel. Ha, ha! we go the gait that leaves no dust behind!"

"There she blows—she blows!—she blows!—right ahead!" was now the mast-head cry.

"Aye, aye!" cried Stubb, "I knew it—ye can't escape—blow on and split your spout, O whale! the mad fiend himself is after ye! blow your trump—blister your lungs!—Ahab will dam off your blood, as a miller shuts his water-gate upon the stream!"

C H A P T E R
THIRTY-TWO

*The Chase—
Second Day*

And Stubb did but speak out for well nigh all that crew. The frenzies of the chase had by this time worked them bubblingly up, like old wine worked anew. The hand of Fate had snatched all their souls; and by the stirring perils of the previous day; the rack of the past night's suspense; the fixed, unfearing, blind, reckless way in which their wild craft went plunging towards its flying mark; by all these things, their hearts were bowled along.

They were one man, not thirty. For as the one ship that held them all; though it was put together of all contrasting things—oak, and maple, and pine wood; iron, and pitch, and hemp—yet all these ran into each other in the one concrete hull, which shot on its way, both balanced and directed by the long central keel; even so, all the individualities of the crew, this man's valor, that man's fear; guilt and guiltlessness, all varieties were welded into oneness, and were all directed to that fatal goal which Ahab their one lord and keel did point to.

The rigging lived. The mast-heads, like the tops of tall palms, were outspreadingly tufted with arms and legs. Clinging to a spar with one hand, some reached forth the other with impatient wavings; others, shading their eyes from the vivid sunlight, sat far out on the rocking yards; all the spars in full bearing of mortals, ready and ripe for their fate. Ah! how they still strove through that infinite blueness to seek out the thing that might destroy them!

"Why sing ye not out for him, if ye see him?" cried Ahab, when, after the lapse of some minutes since the first cry, no more had been heard. "Sway me up, men; ye have been deceived; not Moby Dick casts one odd jet that way, and then disappears."

It was even so; in their headlong eagerness, the men had mistaken some other thing for the whale-spout, as the event itself soon proved; for hardly had Ahab reached his perch; hardly was the rope belayed to its pin on deck, when he struck the key-note to an orchestra, that made the air vibrate as with the combined discharges of rifles. The triumphant halloo of thirty buckskin lungs was heard, as—much nearer to the ship than the place of the imaginary jet, less than a mile ahead—Moby Dick bodily burst into view!

For not by any calm and indolent spoutings; not by the peaceable gush of that mystic fountain in his head, did the White Whale now reveal his vicinity; but by the far more wondrous phenomenon of breaching. Rising with his utmost velocity from the furthest depths, the Sperm Whale thus booms his entire bulk into the pure element of air, and piling up a mountain of dazzling foam, shows his place to the distance of seven miles and more.

"There she breaches! there she breaches!" was the cry, as in his immeasurable bravadoes the White Whale tossed himself salmon-like to Heaven. So suddenly seen in the blue plain of the sea, and relieved against the still bluer margin of the sky, the spray that he raised, for the moment, intolerably glittered and glared like a glacier; and stood there gradually fading and fading away from its first sparkling intensity, to the dim mistiness of an advancing shower in a vale.

"Aye, breach your last to the sun, Moby Dick!" cried Ahab, "thy hour and thy harpoon are at hand!—Down! down all of ye, but one man at the fore. The boats!—stand by!"

Unmindful of the tedious rope-ladders of the shrouds, the men, like shooting stars, slid to the deck, by the isolated backstays and halyards; while Ahab, less dartingly, but still rapidly was dropped from his perch.

"Lower away," he cried, so soon as he had reached his boat—a spare one, rigged the afternoon previous. "Mr. Starbuck, the ship is thine—keep away from the boats, but keep near them. Lower, all!"

As if to strike a quick terror into them, Moby Dick had turned, and was now coming for the three crews. Ahab's boat was central; and cheering his men, he told them he would take the whale head-and-head,—that is, pull straight up to his forehead,—a not uncommon thing. The White Whale churning himself into furious speed, almost in an instant as it were, rushing among the boats with open jaws, and a lashing tail, offered appalling battle on every side; and heedless of the irons darted at him from every boat, seemed only intent on annihilating each separate plank of which those boats were made. But skilfully manœuvred, incessantly wheeling like trained chargers in the field; the boats for a while eluded him; though, at times, but by a plank's breadth; while all the time, Ahab's unearthly slogan tore every other cry but his to shreds.

But at last in his untraceable evolutions, the White Whale so crossed and recrossed, and in a thousand ways entangled the slack of the three lines now fast to him, that they foreshortened, and, of themselves, warped the devoted boats towards the planted irons in him. That instant, the White Whale made a sudden rush among the remaining tangles; irresistibly dragged the boats of Stubb and Flask towards his flukes; dashed them together like two rolling husks on a surf-beaten beach, and then, diving down into the sea, disappeared in a boiling maelstrom.

While the two crews were yet circling in the waters, reaching out after the revolving line-tubs, oars, and other floating furniture, while aslope little Flask bobbed up and down like an empty vial, twitching his legs upwards to escape the dreaded jaws of sharks; and Stubb was lustily singing out for some one to ladle him up; and while the old man's line—now parting—admitted of his pulling into the creamy pool to rescue whom he could;—in that wild simultaneousness of a thousand concreted perils,—Ahab's yet unstricken boat seemed drawn up towards Heaven by invisible wires,—as, arrow-like, shooting perpendicularly from the sea, the White Whale dashed his broad forehead against its bottom, and sent it, turning over and over, into the air; till it fell again—gunwale downwards—and Ahab and his men struggled out from under it, like seals from a sea-side cave.

The first uprising momentum of the whale launched him to a little distance from the centre of the destruction he had made; and with his back to it, he now lay for a moment slowly feeling with his flukes from side to side; and whenever a stray oar, bit of plank, the least chip or crumb of the boats touched his skin, his tail swiftly drew back, and came sideways smiting the sea. But soon, as if satisfied that his work for that time was done, he pushed his pleated forehead through the ocean, and trailing after him the intertangled lines, continued his leeward way at a traveller's methodic pace.

As before, the ship came bearing down to the rescue, and dropping a boat, picked up the floating mariners, tubs, oars, and whatever else could be caught at, and safely landed them on her decks. Some sprained shoulders, wrists, and ankles; livid contusions; wrenched harpoons and lances; inextricable intricacies of rope; shattered oars and planks; all these were there; but no fatal

or even serious ill seemed to have befallen any one. As with Fedallah the day before, so Ahab was now found grimly clinging to his boat's broken half, which afforded a comparatively easy float; nor did it so exhaust him as the previous day's mishap.

But when he was helped to the deck, all eyes were fastened upon him; as instead of standing by himself he still half-hung upon the shoulder of Starbuck, who had thus far been the foremost to assist him. His ivory leg had been snapped off, leaving but one short sharp splinter.

"Oh, oh, oh! how this splinter gores me now! Accursed fate! that the unconquerable captain in the soul should have such a craven mate!"

"Sir?"

"My body, man, not thee. Give me something for a cane—there, that shivered lance will do. Muster the men. Surely I have not seen him yet. By heaven it cannot be!—missing?—quick! call them all."

The old man's hinted thought was true. Upon mustering the company, the Parsee was not there.

"The Parsee!" cried Stubb—"he must have been caught in—"

"The black vomit wrench thee!—run all of ye above, alow, cabin, forecastle—find him—not gone—not gone!"

But quickly they returned to him with the tidings that the Parsee was nowhere to be found.

"Aye, sir," said Stubb—"caught among the tangles of your line—I thought I saw him dragging under."

"*My* line! *my* line? Gone?—gone? The harpoon, too!—d'ye see it?—the forged iron, men, the white whale's—no, no, no,—blistered fool! this hand did dart it!—'tis in the fish!—Aloft there! Keep him nailed—Quick!—all hands to the rigging of the boats—collect the oars—harpooneers! the irons, the irons!—hoist the royals higher—a pull on all the sheets!—helm there! steady, steady for your life! I'll ten times girdle the unmeasured globe; yea and dive straight through it, but I'll slay him yet!"

"Great God! but for one single instant show thyself," cried Starbuck; "never, never wilt thou capture him, old man—In Jesus' name no more of this, that's worse than devil's madness. Two days chased; twice stove to splinters; thy very leg once more snatched from under thee; thy evil shadow gone—all good angels mobbing thee with warnings:—what more wouldst thou have?—Shall we keep chasing this murderous fish till he swamps the last man? Shall we be dragged by him to the bottom of the sea? Shall we be towed by him to the infernal world? Oh, oh,—Impiety and blasphemy to hunt him more!"

"Starbuck, of late I've felt strangely moved to thee. But in this matter of the whale, be the front of thy face to me as the palm of this hand—a lipless, unfeatured blank. Ahab is for ever Ahab, man. This whole act's immutably decreed. 'Twas rehearsed by thee and me a billion years before this ocean rolled. Fool! I am the Fates' lieutenant; I act under orders. Look thou, underling! that thou obeyest mine.—Stand round me, men. Ye see an old man cut down to the stump; leaning on a shivered lance; propped up on a lonely foot. 'Tis Ahab—his body's part; but Ahab's soul's a centipede, that moves upon a hundred legs. I feel strained, half stranded; and I may look so. But ere I break, ye'll hear me crack; and till ye hear *that*, know that Ahab's hawser tows his purpose yet. Believe ye, men, in the things called omens? Then laugh aloud, and cry encore! For ere they drown, drowning things will twice rise to the surface; then rise again, to sink for evermore. So with Moby Dick—two days he's floated—to-morrow will be the third. Aye, men, he'll rise once more,—but only to spout his last! D'ye feel brave, men, brave?"

"As fearless fire," cried Stubb.

"And as mechanical," muttered Ahab. Then as the men went forward, he muttered on:—"The things called omens!—The Parsee—the Parsee!—gone, gone? and he was to go before:—but still was to be seen again ere I could perish—How's that?—There's a riddle now might baffle all the lawyers backed by the ghosts of the whole line of judges:—like a hawk's beak it pecks my brain. *I'll, I'll* solve it, though!"

When dusk descended, the whale was still in sight to leeward.

So once more the sail was shortened, and everything passed nearly as on the previous night; only, the sound of hammers, and the hum of the grindstone was heard till nearly daylight, as the men toiled by lanterns in the complete and careful rigging of the spare boats and sharpening their fresh weapons for the morrow. Meantime, of the broken keel of Ahab's wrecked craft the carpenter made him another leg; while still as on the night before, slouched Ahab stood fixed within his scuttle.

The morning of the third day dawned fair and fresh, and once more the solitary night-man at the fore-mast-head was relieved by crowds of the daylight look-outs, who dotted every mast and almost every spar.

"D'ye see him?" cried Ahab. "Aloft there! What d'ye see?"

"Nothing, sir."

"Nothing! The doubloon goes a-begging! See the sun! Aye, aye, it must be so. I've oversailed him. How, got the start? Aye, he's chasing *me* now; not I, *him*—that's bad; I might have known it, too. Fool! the lines—the harpoons he's towing. Aye, aye, I have run him by last night. About! about! Come down, all of ye, but the regular look outs! Man the braces!"

CHAPTER
THIRTY-THREE

*The Chase—
Third Day*

Steering as she had done, the wind had been somewhat on the Pequod's quarter, so that now being pointed in the reverse direction, the braced ship sailed hard upon the breeze as she rechurned the cream in her own white wake.

"Against the wind he now steers for the open jaw," murmured Starbuck to himself. "God keep us, but already my bones feel damp within me, and from the inside wet my flesh. I misdoubt me that I disobey my God in obeying him!"

"Stand by to sway me up!" cried Ahab, advancing to the hempen basket. "We should meet him soon."

"Aye, aye, sir," and straightway Starbuck did Ahab's bidding, and once more Ahab swung on high.

A whole hour now passed; gold-beaten out to ages. Time itself now held long breaths with keen suspense. But at last, some three points off the weather bow, Ahab descried the spout again, and instantly from the three mast-heads three shrieks went up as if the tongues of fire had voiced it.

"Forehead to forehead I meet thee, this third time, Moby Dick! On deck there!—brace sharper up; crowd her into the wind's eye. He's too far off to lower yet, Mr. Starbuck. The sails shake! Stand over that helmsman with a top-maul! So, so; he travels fast, and I must down. But let me have one more good round look aloft here at the sea; there's time for that. What's that he said? he should still go before me, my pilot; and yet to be seen again? But where? Will I have eyes at the bottom of the sea, supposing I descend those stairs? and all night I've been sailing from him, wherever he did sink to. Aye, aye, like many more thou told'st direful truth as touching thyself, O Parsee; but, Ahab, there thy shot fell short. Good by, mast-head—keep a good eye upon the whale, the while I'm gone. We'll talk to-morrow, nay, to-night, when the white whale lies down there, tied by head and tail."

He gave the word; and still gazing round him, was steadily lowered through the cloven blue air to the deck.

In due time the boats were lowered; but as standing in his shallop's stern, Ahab just hovered upon the point of the descent, he waved to the mate,—who held one of the tackle-ropes on deck—and bade him pause.

"Starbuck!"

"Sir?"

"For the third time my soul's ship starts upon this voyage, Starbuck."

"Aye, sir, thou wilt have it so."

"Some ships sail from their ports, and ever afterwards are missing, Starbuck!"

"Truth, sir: saddest truth."

"Some men die at ebb tide; some at low water; some at the full of the flood:—and I feel now like a billow that's all one crested comb, Starbuck. I am old;—shake hands with me, man."

Their hands met; their eyes fastened; Starbuck's tears the glue.
"Oh, my captain, my captain!—noble heart—go not—
go not!—see, it's a brave man that weeps;
how great the agony of the persuasion then!"
"Lower away!"—cried Ahab, tossing
the mate's arm from him.
"Stand by the crew!"
In an instant the boat was
pulling round close under the stern.
"The sharks! the sharks!" cried a
voice from the low cabin-window there;
"O master, my master, come back!"
But Ahab heard nothing; for his
own voice was high-lifted then;
and the boat leaped on.
Yet the voice spake true;
for scarce had he pushed from
the ship, when numbers of sharks,
seemingly rising from out the dark
waters beneath the hull, maliciously
snapped at the blades of the oars,
and in this way accompanied
the boat with their bites.

"Heart of wrought steel!" murmured Starbuck gazing over the side, and following with his eyes the receding boat. "Oh! my God! what is this that shoots through me, and leaves me so deadly calm, yet expectant. Future things swim before me, as in empty outlines and skeletons; all the past is somehow grown dim. Mary, girl! thou fadest in pale glories behind me; boy! I seem to see but thy eyes grown wondrous blue. Strangest problems of life seem clearing; but clouds sweep between—Is my journey's end coming? My legs feel faint; like his who has footed it all day. Feel thy heart,—beats it yet—Stir thyself, Starbuck!—stave it off—move, move! speak aloud!—Mast-head there! See ye my boy's hand on the hill?—Crazed;—aloft there!—keep thy keenest eye upon the boats:—mark well the whale!—Ho! again!—drive off that hawk! see! he pecks—he tears the vane"—pointing to the red flag flying at the main-truck—"Ha! he soars away with it!—Where's the old man now? see'st thou that sight, oh Ahab!—shudder, shudder!"

The boats had not gone very far, when by a signal from the mast-heads—a downward pointed arm, Ahab knew that the whale had sounded; but intending to be near him at the next rising, he held on his way a little sideways from the vessel; the becharmed crew maintaining the profoundest silence, as the head-beat waves hammered and hammered against the opposing bow.

"Drive, drive in your nails, oh ye waves! to their uttermost heads drive them in! ye but strike a thing without a lid; and no coffin and no hearse can be mine:—and hemp only can kill me! Ha! ha!"

Suddenly the waters around them slowly swelled in broad circles; then quickly upheaved, as if sideways sliding from a submerged berg of ice, swiftly rising to the surface. A low rumbling sound was heard; a subterranean hum; and then all held their breaths; as bedraggled with trailing ropes, and harpoons, and lances, a vast form shot lengthwise, but obliquely from the sea. Shrouded in a thin drooping veil of mist, it hovered for a moment in the rainbowed air; and then fell swamping back into the deep. Crushed thirty feet upwards, the waters flashed for an instant like heaps of fountains, then brokenly sank in a shower of flakes, leaving the circling surface creamed like new milk round the marble trunk of the whale.

"Give way!" cried Ahab to the oarsmen, and the boats darted forward to the attack; but maddened by yesterday's fresh irons that corroded in him, Moby Dick seemed combinedly possessed by all the angels that fell from heaven. The wide tiers of welded tendons overspreading his broad white forehead, beneath the transparent skin, looked knitted together; as head on, he came churning his tail among the boats; and once more flailed them apart; spilling out the irons and lances from the two mates' boats, and dashing in one side of the upper part of their bows, but leaving Ahab's almost without a scar.

While Daggoo and Tashtego were stopping the strained planks; and as the whale swimming out from them, turned, and showed one entire flank as he shot by them again; at that moment a quick cry went up. Lashed round and round to the fish's back; pinioned in the turns upon turns in which, during the past night, the whale had reeled the involutions of the lines around him, the half torn body of the Parsee was seen; his sable raiment frayed to shreds; his distended eyes turned full upon old Ahab.

The harpoon dropped from his hand.

"Befooled, befooled! Aye, Parsee! I see thee again.—Aye, and thou goest before; and this, *this* then is the hearse that thou didst promise. But I hold thee to the last letter of thy word. Where is the second hearse? Away, mates, to the ship! those boats are useless now; repair them if ye can in time, and return to me; if not, Ahab is enough to die—Down, men! the first thing that but offers to jump from this boat I stand in, that thing I harpoon.

Ye are not other men, but my arms and my legs; and so obey me.—Where's the whale? gone down again?"

But he looked too nigh the boat; for Moby Dick was now again steadily swimming forward; and had almost passed the ship. He seemed swimming with his utmost velocity, and only intent upon pursuing his own straight path.

"Oh! Ahab," cried Starbuck, "not too late is it, even now, the third day, to desist. See! Moby Dick seeks thee not. It is thou, thou, that madly seekest him!"

Setting sail to the rising wind, the lonely boat was swiftly impelled to leeward, by both oars and canvas. And at last when Ahab was sliding by the vessel, so near as plainly to distinguish Starbuck's face as he leaned over the rail, he hailed him to turn the vessel about, and follow him, not too swiftly, at a judicious interval. Glancing upwards, he saw Tashtego, Queequeg, and Daggoo, eagerly mounting to the three mast-heads; while the oarsmen were rocking in the two staved boats which had but just been hoisted to the side, and were busily at work in repairing them. And now marking that the vane or flag was gone from the main-mast-head, he shouted to Tashtego, who had just gained that perch, to descend again for another flag, and a hammer and nails, and so nail it to the mast.

Whether fagged by the three days' running chase, and the resistance to his swimming in the knotted hamper he bore; or whether it was some latent deceitfulness and malice in him: whichever was true, the White Whale's way now began to abate, as it seemed, from the boat so rapidly nearing him once more; though indeed the whale's last start had not been so long a one as before. And still as Ahab glided over the waves the unpitying sharks accompanied him; and so pertinaciously stuck to the boat; and so continually bit at the plying oars, that the blades became jagged and crunched, and left small splinters in the sea, at almost every dip.

"Heed them not! those teeth but give new rowlocks to your oars. Pull on! 'tis the better rest, the shark's jaw than the yielding water."

"But at every bite, sir, the thin blades grow smaller and smaller!"

"They will last long enough! pull on!—But who can tell"—he muttered—"whether these sharks swim to feast on the whale or on Ahab?—But pull on! Aye, all alive, now—we near him. The helm! take the helm; let me pass,"—and so saying, two of the oarsmen helped him forward to the bows of the still flying boat.

At length as the craft was cast to one side, and ran ranging along with the White Whale's flank, he seemed strangely oblivious of its advance—as the whale sometimes will—and Ahab was fairly within the smoky mountain mist, which, thrown off from the whale's spout, curled round his great hump; he was even thus close to him; when, with body arched back, and both arms lengthwise high-lifted to the poise, he darted his fierce iron, and his far fiercer curse into the hated whale. As both steel and curse sank to the socket, as if sucked into a morass, Moby Dick sideways writhed; spasmodically rolled his nigh flank against the bow, and, without staving a hole in it, so suddenly canted the boat over, that had it not been for the elevated part of the gunwale to which he then clung, Ahab would once more have been tossed into the sea. As it was, three of the oarsmen were flung out; but so fell, that, in an instant two of them clutched the gunwale again, and rising to its level on a combing wave, hurled themselves bodily inboard again; the third man helplessly dropping astern, but still afloat and swimming.

Almost simultaneously, with a mighty volition of ungraduated, instantaneous swiftness, the White Whale darted through the weltering sea.

But when Ahab cried out to the steersman to take new turns with the line, and hold it so; and commanded the crew to turn round on their seats, and tow the boat up to the mark; it snapped in the empty air!

"What breaks in me? Some sinew cracks!—'tis whole again; oars! oars! Burst in upon him!"

Hearing the tremendous rush of the sea-crashing boat, the whale wheeled round to present his blank forehead at bay; but in that evolution, catching sight of the nearing black hull of the ship; seemingly seeing in it the source of all his persecutions; of a sudden, he bore down upon its advancing prow, smiting his jaws amid fiery showers of foam.

Ahab staggered; his hand smote his forehead. "I grow blind; hands! stretch out before me that I may yet grope my way. Is't night?"

"The whale! The ship!" cried the cringing oarsmen.

"Oars! oars! I see: the ship! the ship! Dash on, my men! Will ye not save my ship?"

But as the oarsmen violently forced their boat through the sledge-hammering seas, the before whale-smitten bow-ends of two planks burst through, and in an instant almost, the temporarily disabled boat lay nearly level with the waves; its half-wading, splashing crew, trying hard to stop the gap and bale out the pouring water.

Meantime, for that one beholding instant, Tashtego's mast-head hammer remained suspended in his hand; and the red flag, half-wrapping him as with a plaid, then streamed itself straight out from him, as his own forward-flowing heart; while Starbuck and Stubb, standing upon the bowsprit beneath, caught sight of the down-coming monster just as soon as he.

"The whale, the whale! Up helm, up helm! oh, all ye sweet powers of air, now hug me close! Let not Starbuck die, if die he must, in a woman's fainting fit.

Up helm, I say—ye fools, the jaw! the jaw! Is this the end of all my bursting prayers? all my life-long fidelities? Oh, Ahab, Ahab, lo, thy work. Steady! helmsman, steady. Nay, nay! Up helm again! He turns to meet us! Oh, his unappeasable brow drives on towards one, whose duty tells him he cannot depart. My God, stand by me now!"

From the ship's bows, nearly all the seamen now hung inactive; hammers, bits of plank, lances, and harpoons, mechanically retained in their hands, just as they had darted from their various employments; all their enchanted eyes intent upon the whale, which from side to side strangely vibrating his predestinating head, sent a broad band of overspreading semicircular foam before him as he rushed. Retribution, swift vengeance, eternal malice were in his whole aspect, and spite of all that mortal man could do, the solid white buttress of his forehead smote the ship's starboard bow, till men and timbers reeled. Some fell flat upon their faces. Like dislodged trucks, the heads of the harpooneers aloft shook on their bull-like necks. Through the breach, they heard the waters pour, as mountain torrents down a flume.

"The ship! The hearse!—the second hearse!" cried Ahab from the boat; "its wood could only be American!"

Diving beneath the settling ship, the whale ran quivering along its keel; but turning under water, swiftly shot to the surface again, far off the other bow, but within a few yards of Ahab's boat, where, for a time, he lay quiescent.

"I turn my body from the sun. What ho, Tashtego! let me hear thy hammer. Oh! death-glorious ship! must ye then perish, and without me? Am I cut off from the last fond pride of meanest shipwrecked captains? Oh, lonely death on lonely life! Oh, now I feel my topmost greatness lies in my topmost grief. Ho, ho! from all your furthest bounds, pour ye now in, ye bold billows of my whole foregone life, and top this one piled comber of my death!

Towards thee I roll, thou all-destroying but unconquering whale; to the last I grapple with thee; from hell's heart I stab at thee; for hate's sake I spit my last breath at thee. Sink all coffins and all hearses to one common pool! and since neither can be mine, let me then tow to pieces, while still chasing thee, though tied to thee, thou damned whale! *Thus*, I give up the spear!"

The harpoon was darted; the stricken whale flew forward; with igniting velocity the line ran through the groove;—ran foul. Ahab stooped to clear it; he did clear it; but the flying turn caught him round the neck, and voicelessly as Turkish mutes bowstring their victim, he was shot out of the boat, ere the crew knew he was gone.

Next instant, the heavy eye-splice in the rope's final end flew out of the stark-empty tub, knocked down an oarsman, and smiting the sea, disappeared in its depths.

For an instant, the tranced boat's crew stood still; then turned. "The ship? Great God, where is the ship?" Soon they saw her fading phantom; only the uppermost masts out of the water; while fixed by infatuation, or fidelity, or fate, to their once lofty perches, the pagan harpooneers still maintained their sinking lookouts on the sea. And now, concentric circles seized the lone boat itself, and all its crew, and each floating oar, and every lance-pole, and spinning, animate and inanimate, all round and round in one vortex, carried the smallest chip of the Pequod out of sight.

But as the last whelmings intermixingly poured themselves over the sunken head of the Indian at the mainmast, leaving a few inches of the erect spar yet visible, together with long streaming yards of the flag;—at that instant, a red arm and a hammer hovered backwardly uplifted in the open air, in the act of nailing the flag to the subsiding spar. A sky-hawk that tauntingly had followed the main-truck downwards; this bird

now chanced to intercept its broad fluttering wing between the
hammer and the wood; the submerged savage beneath,
in his death-grasp, kept his hammer frozen there; and
so the bird of heaven, with archangelic shrieks, and his whole
captive form folded in the flag of Ahab, went down with
this ship, which, like Satan, would not sink to hell till she
had dragged a living part of heaven along with her, and
helmeted herself with it.

Now small fowls flew screaming over the yet yawning
gulf; a sullen white surf beat against its steep sides;
then all collapsed, and the great shroud
of the sea rolled on as it rolled
five thousand years ago.

EPILOGUE

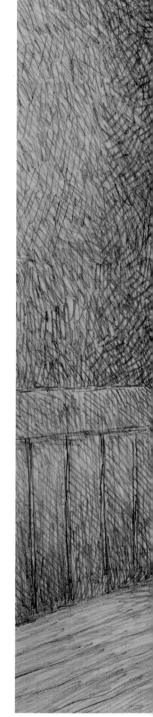

"*And I Only Am Escaped Alone to Tell Thee.*"

—*Job*

THE DRAMA'S DONE. Why then here does any one step forth?—Because one did survive the wreck. It so chanced, that after the Parsee's disappearance, I was he whom the Fates ordained to take the place of Ahab's bowsman, when that bowsman assumed the vacant post; the same, who, when on the last day the three men were tossed from out the rocking boat, was dropped astern. So, floating on the margin of the ensuing scene, and in full sight of it, when the half-spent suction of the sunk ship reached me, I was then, but slowly, drawn towards the closing vortex. When I reached it, it had subsided to a creamy pool. Round and round, then, and ever contracting towards the button-like black bubble at the axis of that slowly wheeling circle, like another Ixion I did revolve. Till, gaining that vital centre, the black bubble upward burst; and now, liberated by reason of its cunning spring, and, owing to its great buoyancy, rising with great force, the coffin life-buoy shot lengthwise from the sea, fell over, and floated by my side. Buoyed up by that coffin, for almost one whole day and night, I floated on a soft and dirge-like main. The unharming sharks, they glided by as if with padlocks on their mouths; the savage sea-hawks sailed with sheathed beaks. On the second day, a sail drew near, nearer, and picked me up at last. It was the devious-cruising Rachel, that in her retracing search after her missing children, only found another orphan.

FINIS

Glossary

A

ABAFT
behind, toward the stern
(back) of the boat

ABOVE HATCHES
on deck, opposite of *below*
or *down below*

AFT
toward the stern

ARCHIPELAGOS
groups of islands

ASTERN
an order to row
backwards;
behind

ATHWART
across

AUGER
a carpenter's tool for
boring holes

B

BACKSTAYS
ropes that support masts
from behind

BACK THE MAIN YARD
an order to adjust sails to stop
or slow a ship

BACK WATER
an order to row astern

BANDS
ropes that hold something
in position

BARE-POLED
with no sails up

BEAM
side, as in *lee* or *weather beam*

BEND
to fix a sail to a yard or mast

BINNACLE
a box or container that holds
the steering compass

BLOCK
a wooden pulley

BLUBBER
the fatty part of a whale's
body; boiled down, it
produces whale oil

BOW
the front part of a ship or boat

BOWSMAN
the crewman who pulls
the bow oar

BRACES
the ropes by which a
yard is swung, or trimmed,
to catch the wind

BREAKER
a small barrel

BREAK OUT
to open, get, or empty

BULWARKS
wooden wall enclosing
deck along ship's side

BUSHEL
a measure of
capacity
equaling eight
gallons

C

CAPSIZE
turn over

CAPSTAN
a vertical windlass, or
winch, for hauling ropes

CAPSTAN HEAD
the top of the capstan

CAREEN
to haul a ship onto
her side

CAULK THE SEAMS
to force waterproofing
material into the gaps
between the planks of
a ship

CHART
sea map

CLOSE REEF
reduce the amount of sail
for heavy weather

CLUMSY CLEAT
a knee rest in a whaleboat
to aid the harpooner's balance

CORDAGE
ropes and rigging

CRANE
angled device to hang
whaleboats from a ship's side;
also called davits

CROSSTREES
fixed beams at mastheads

CRUISING GROUND
hunting ground

D

DOUBLOON
a gold coin

DOUGHBOY
the traditional American
name for a ship's steward

E

EYE SPLICE
a loop spliced into a rope

F

FLUKE
the outer part of a whale's
tail, as in "There go flukes."

FLUME
a water chute or channel

FORE

forward

FORECASTLE

the bow section where

the crew lives

FURL

to take in a sail by

gathering it up, usually

to a yard

G

GALLOWS

a structure for hanging

things (and men) from

GROG

liquor

GROUND-TIER BUTTS

the bottom level of

barrels in the hold

GUNWALE

the wooden edge or rim

of a ship or boat

H

HALYARD

rope used to raise

or lower sails

HANDS

seamen or sailors

HARPOON

barbed spear thrown

into a whale to attach

a whaleboat to it

HATCHES

openings in the deck

HEADSMEN

men who took the bow

position in a whaleboat

HELM see **tiller**

HEMP

a strong, dark rope;

hangmen use it

HOLD

the storage area

below deck

HOLDER

a crewman who

works in the hold

HOOPS

metal rings holding

a barrel's staves

together

J

JIB

triangular sail carried

at the fore end

JUNK

a type of boat or ship

K

KEEL

the bottom of a ship, sometimes

a term for a ship or a boat

L

LANCE

a spear without a barb, thrust

into a whale to kill it

LARBOARD

the left-hand side

of a ship or boat

LEE, LEEWARD

the side of a vessel away

from the wind

LEES

dregs or leavings of beer

or wine

LEVIATHAN

a whale

LIGHTNING-ROD-END

the chain end of

a lightning conductor that

dangles in the sea

LINE

rope

LINE TUB

a half barrel that holds

coiled harpoon line

LOADSTONE,

or **LODESTONE**

a geological material with

magnetic properties

LOG

a navigational aid to estimate

speed and distance

LOGGERHEAD

a post on a whaleboat

LOOM

to come into sight; also the

handle end of an oar

LOWERING

putting whaleboats in the

water to start the chase; also

gloomy, cloudy weather

LOWER SAIL

to bring sail down

LUBBER

a useless seaman;

or a land person

M

MAIN-CHAINS

where the main shrouds

join the side of the ship

MAINTOP

the platform at the top

of the first part of the

mainmast

MAST

The *Pequod* had three — fore, main, and mizzen. The first part of each was called the mast (or lower mast), above that was the topmast, and then came the topgallant and, on some ships, the royal mast.

MASTHEAD

place on a mast where lookouts perch; also the lookouts themselves

MATCH KEG

a waterproof container for matches

MEASURE

a small pewter cup that measures portions of liquor

OFFING

the near distance

OIL JACKET

a tarpaulin or an oilskin coat

PARMACETTI

whalers' name for a whale; from *spermaceti*

PAY WITH PITCH

to waterproof seams with pitch (a tarry substance)

PROW

the bow or front of a ship

Q

QUADRANT

an instrument for measuring navigation angles

QUARTER

either back corner of a ship

QUARTER BOAT

the whaleboat hanging on a ship's quarter

QUARTERDECK

the rear part of a ship's deck; officers' territory

R

RACK

flying foam

RECALL SIGNALS

flags flown to call whale-boats back to the ship

REEF

to reduce the size of a sail

RIGGING

ropes and gear that hold the masts up and control sails

RINGBOLTS

rings fixed in the deck for fastening

ROWLOCKS

notches in a boat's gunwale in which oars may pivot

ROYAL

third mast up from the deck; also the sail rigged on that mast

SCUD

flying foam

SCUTTLE

an opening or hatch in the deck; some have a surrounding wall or frame

SHEAVE

the wheel inside a block

SHEETS

the ropes at the corners of a square sail to haul it tight

SHROUDS

the rigging that holds masts up

SOMERSET

somersault

SOUND

to dive; also to measure depth in water

SPOUT

the visible cloud of vapor that forms as a whale breathes

SPOUT HOLE

the breathing hole in the top part of a whale

SPADES

spade-shaped cutting implements

SPAR

a wooden yard or boom, usually to hold a sail

SPLICE

to join ropes by interweaving their strands together

SQUARE THE YARDS

adjust ("trim") yards to catch the wind

STARBOARD

the right-hand side of a ship or boat

STAVE

to break in; or a shaped piece of wood

STAYS

ropes that strengthen or support

STEERING OAR

Whaleboats had no tiller or rudder, so were steered with an oar over the stern.

STERN

the back of a boat or ship

STEWARD

captain and officers' servant

STOVE

broken in

STOWAGE

putting away or storing

STRIKE

to lower or bring down

STUNSAIL, STUNS'L

a lightweight sail rigged outside the mainsails in calm weather

TACK

part of a sail; to sail in zigzags

TACKLE

a collection of blocks and rope for pulling and lifting

TAFFRAIL

the rail or bulwark at the aft end of the ship

TARPAULIN

a waterproof hat or jacket; also a sheet of heavy cloth

TEMPER

to harden metal by dousing it in liquid

"THERE GO FLUKES!"

a shout indicating that a whale is diving

"THERE SHE BLOWS!"

a shout indicating that a whale spout has been seen

THWART

a seat across a boat

TILLER

the bar that moves the rudder to steer the ship

TOPGALLANT

the sail carried on the topgallant mast

TOP-HAMPER

masts, spars, and rigging above the decks

TOP-MAUL

a type of hammer

TRANSOM

the strengthening beam of wood across the stern of the main cabin

TRUCK

the wooden disc forming a weatherproof cap at the masthead

TRUMPET

a megaphone

TRY-POTS, TRYWORKS

equipment for rendering whale blubber into oil

TURK'S HEAD

a large ornamental knot

UP HELM

an order to steer off the wind, which will speed up a ship

VANE

a flag or streamer

WAIF-POLE

a pole with a flag on it to mark an abandoned whale

WATCHES

four-hour periods of work time on board a ship

WEATHER

the side of a vessel toward the wind; the opposite of *lee*

WEATHER BOW

the side of a ship's bow that is toward the wind

WHALER

a ship or man who hunts whales

WINDLASS

a winch turned by long wooden bars called handspikes, used for hauling heavy objects and anchors

WINDWARD

the opposite of *leeward*

YARD

a spar hung crosswise on the masts, with sails bent on

YAW

to move in a zigzag motion; also to wander about

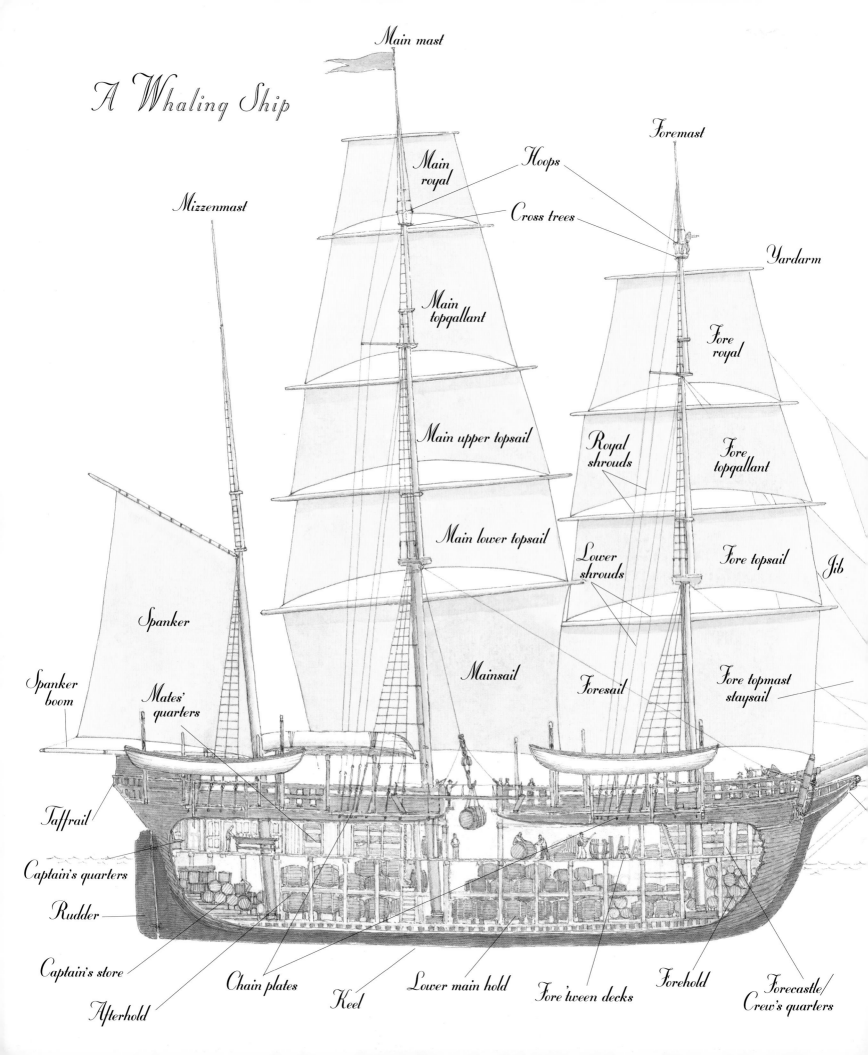

A Whaling Ship

Main mast

Mizzenmast

Foremast

Main royal

Hoops

Cross trees

Yardarm

Main topgallant

Fore royal

Royal shrouds

Fore topgallant

Main upper topsail

Main lower topsail

Lower shrouds

Fore topsail

Jib

Spanker

Mainsail

Foresail

Fore topmast staysail

Spanker boom

Mates' quarters

Taffrail

Captain's quarters

Rudder

Captain's store

Chain plates

Afterhold

Keel

Lower main hold

Fore 'tween decks

Forehold

Forecastle/ Crew's quarters

Whaling Ship Deck

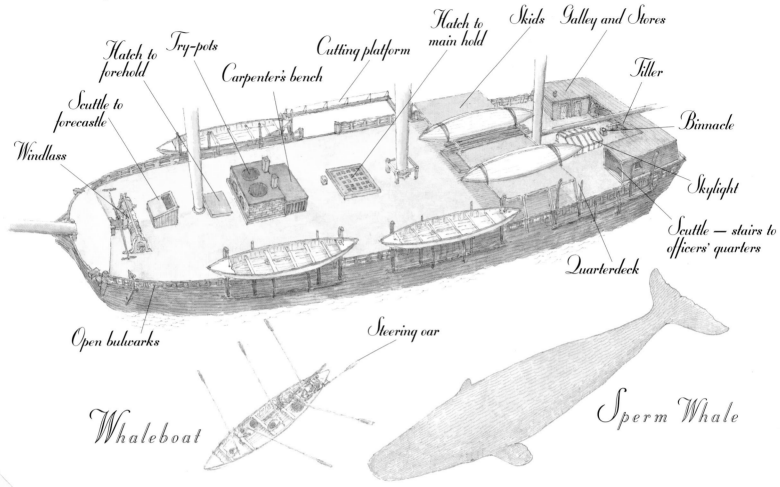

Hatch to forehold

Try-pots

Carpenter's bench

Cutting platform

Hatch to main hold

Skids

Galley and Stores

Tiller

Scuttle to forecastle

Binnacle

Windlass

Skylight

Scuttle — stairs to officers' quarters

Quarterdeck

Open bulwarks

Steering oar

Whaleboat

Sperm Whale

Flying jib

Bowsprit

Martingale

Fiddlehead

A whaling ship was around 110 feet (33 meters) long and a whaleboat around 26 feet (7 meters) long. The average length of an adult male sperm whale is 60 feet (18 meters), although much larger whales were caught, measuring up to 100 feet (30 meters) in length.

"In token of my admiration for his genius,
this book is inscribed to Nathaniel Hawthorne" ⸺ HM

For my mother, Dot
And in memory of my friend Jan Mark, 1943–2006 ⸺ JN

For Augusta and Barnaby ⸺ PB

Abridgement copyright © 2006 by Jan Needle   Illustrations copyright © 2006 by Patrick Benson

First U.S. edition 2006

Library of Congress Cataloging-in-Publication Data is available.

Library of Congress Catalog Card Number pending

ISBN-13: 978-0-7636-3018-8
ISBN-10: 0-7636-3018-7

2 4 6 8 10 9 7 5 3 1

Printed in the United States of America

This book was typeset in Historical-Fell Roman, Cold Mountain, and Stuyvesant.
The illustrations were done in pencil, ink, and watercolor.

Candlewick Press
2067 Massachusetts Avenue
Cambridge, Massachusetts, 02140

visit us at www.candlewick.com